HER ARTIST

AIDEN

JB TREPAGNIER

Her Artist Copyright © 2018 JB Trepagnier

All Rights Reserved. No part of this publication may be reproduced, stored in a retrieval system, or transmitted, in any form or in any means – by electronic, mechanical, photocopying, recording, or otherwise without prior written permission

Cover by Hannah Stern-Jacob Designs

 Created with Vellum

As much as I wanted the beautiful gray-eyed girl at the salon to come home with me, I was sure it wasn't going to happen. I had a feeling she was running from something big and it turned out I was right. She had no reason to trust me and it seemed like I got on her nerves. I was also pretty sure when I went home and told the guys I wanted her to live with us, they were going to tell me no. I was right about that too.

I was trying not to get angry when they were treating her like some stray dog I was taking in again. I'd bonded with one when we were overseas and I'd done everything I could to take him home with me, but I could never get anything approved to bring him to America. I'd raised the funds, but no one would approve the paperwork.

Misty wasn't a dog, pet, or stray. There was just something about her that called to my soul. It made me want to protect her, no matter what it was she was running from. I knew my friends liked her too. I'd never fought over a girl with any of them before like Gareth and Casey had. I knew when we came to our agreement, Misty was nothing like Iris. I'd always thought Iris was a little silly and not worth their attention.

Misty could be silly when she wanted to be and she had this combination of sexy pinup girl after she agreed to my makeover suggestion and innocent adorableness. Misty was far from innocent. At least, not that first day in my room alone with her. Her eyes grew to the size of saucers when she saw me in my towel and I thought I might have to take my time with her because she didn't have a lot of experience. It turned out she had been wondering what was underneath my towel the entire time she was staring at me like a deer in headlights.

After talking with her more, I knew she didn't have a lot of experience. She'd dated some total asshole in college who didn't care if she enjoyed it or not and wasn't very adventurous. She really came alive with us. Well, and with me in my bedroom that first day alone with her. Her ex had to be pretty stupid to not realized what was sitting right in front of him. Misty was curious, responsive, and just an amazing girl all around.

I don't think she realized how much it meant to me that she asked me to give her the first tattoo she would have. I was only giving her a hard time when I told her she should get full sleeves at the salon. I knew they would look good on her, but I never thought she would go for it. When she asked, I knew it had to be special. I could have given her angel wings since she was an angel to everyone in the house. I gave her dragonfly wings instead of because she looked like some sort of fae.

I'll never forgive myself for what we did to her when she got home after being kidnapped. She needed us and we utterly abandoned her. We fought over her and nearly drove her away. I even punched Gareth in the stomach and that wasn't like me. Andre and I broke an expensive vase when he tackled me when we were fighting over her. I know she heard all the screaming and crashing in the living room.

I don't know what I would have done if we hadn't caught her when she was trying to sneak out the house in the middle of the night. We intended to talk to her in the morning and tell her what we agreed on. I had no idea if she would go for it, but I hoped she would hear us out. I wasn't sure *I* was going for it. I didn't like the idea of sharing her with my friends at first.

I'll never forget the look on her face when I kicked her door down when we heard crashes from her room the night she was going to run. Her face was red and tear stained. I was responsible for that and I never wanted to make her cry. When I saw how upset she was, I just wanted to run to her and hold her. The problem was, everyone else in the room did too and if I made a move, they would too. We'd just start punching each other again and she'd be out the door.

I was a combat medic when I was in the military and seen all kind of horrible shit. I'd rushed out in gunfire to grab a wounded comrade. I never hesitated. But stayed rooted to the spot and not going to Misty when her face was streaked with tears was one of the hardest things I'd ever done. Waiting for one of us to get the words out was second hardest. I wasn't sure if she'd hear us out after our behavior.

I thought for sure she was going to slap all of us in the face and storm out when Gareth suggested we break our no sex rule together. He said we talked about that together and we totally didn't. We never talked about what would happen if she said yes. I think everyone but Gareth was just thinking it would go back to how we were doing it with our days alone with her, but we could break the no sex rule.

I can't say it didn't shock me that came out of Gareth's mouth. He usually said the first thing that popped into his head and he probably just blurted it out when she asked about it. I was about to yank Gareth out the room and apologize to Misty, but she actually perked up and agreed to it. I had no idea that little adorable girl from the salon was that kinky, but when she looked like she really wanted to do it, I found myself with the biggest erection I'd had since I laid eyes on that woman.

I wasn't going to try to dictate what happened. That wasn't anything that had ever happened in any of my fantasies. Multiple women, sure. A woman I loved with my three best friends? That was never a blip on my radar. I was tense and I could tell Misty was nervous too. I knew Casey would be horribly embarrassed and could storm out the room. I suggested we all do a striptease for her just to delay what we were going to do because I was nervous as hell and it looked like Misty was too.

I'd like to say I'd never done a strip tease for a woman before and Misty was the first, but that was a lie. I was almost ninety-nine percent sure the same was true for Gareth. I wouldn't put it past Andre either. I just knew Casey had never done it. I took him for someone who had sex with the lights off until that night on the sectional.

Even though I'd done it before, doing it for Misty was a huge turn on. I intended to let her dictate that night, but when the music ended, I couldn't help being drawn to the sectional and Misty. I asked her to come to me, but let her do what she wished when she did. She jumped in my lap and slowly slid down my dick.

I thought that was the best thing I'd ever felt in my life until I felt Casey behind her and her breasts were pressed into my face so she could suck Gareth off. I loved everything about that girl. Spending time alone with her, sharing her with my friends. No one had ever made me feel as whole as Misty did.

I was painting more than ever and even had several sculptures going on in my studio. Misty was still posing for me, but not all of them were of her. I was no good for Casey's whole investigation. I knew nothing about hacking or being a detective. I stayed with them for moral support and sometimes I did contribute an idea they hadn't thought up yet. I'd sit with them feeling mostly useless at protecting Misty.

If she left to go be with one of the others or we didn't all sleep on the sectional together, I'd stay up for most of the night furiously painting or making art. It wasn't just that I had so many ideas now. I was frustrated. I could handle myself in a fight and could protect Misty if someone somehow managed to get in the house again.

I could do nothing in this chess game we'd gotten ourselves involved in. I could help Casey recover from Serena's little bomb, but I couldn't hunt Serena or Rook like the others could. Hell, I couldn't even play a game of strip chess with Misty like Andre could. Casey had gotten an untraceable text from Rook that we'd meddled enough in his little chess game. Serena was the queen on his board, even if we didn't know what that meant. His queen was now in a bad position on the board and Gareth took away his safe houses.

He'd threatened to take our queen. We'd have to figure out what Rook's big game was and who he was before he found a way to get Misty. He had cops as players on his board. We had to end this game before he got Misty.

2

Casey had always been an awful patient when he was hurt. He'd been shot at work before and I treated him at home for that too. He hated being benched for injuries, but refused to go to the doctor so he could get better. He'd insist I treat him, but he would complain the entire time his recovery wasn't going fast enough.

He wasn't doing that this time, since he got caught in Serena's bomb blast. I suspected that wasn't because he'd grown up a little and realized injuries healed on their own time or that fucking temper on him had lessened. He was doing it because I had Misty helping me this time. She really was having a positive effect on him and the isolation he liked to put himself through instead of talking things out. As I was checking out the bruises on his back and sides, I tried to tell myself she was making him a better patient too.

Casey was lucky to get away with horrible bruising and a few cuts. I'd talked to his physician when we got the call he was injured. The bruising was so bad, they were sure he had internal bleeding and broken ribs. He must have had a little angel on his shoulder that day. His back and sides were garish hues of purple and black and he probably hurt like hell, but he wasn't in for a super long recovery and I didn't have to do physical therapy with him this time. He bitched endlessly through that.

I worked through the night on a sculpture again. I'd probably never sleep again until my friends found Rook and brought down his entire chess board. I wasn't tired. I had this frenetic, manic energy I was running off of. I knew it wasn't going to last. I'd eventually get sick doing this. I knew I needed to stop because I couldn't protect Misty if I was laid up flat on my ass, but I just couldn't sleep.

I was trying. I'd lay in my bed staring at the ceiling with awful thoughts about what Rook would do if he got his hands on Misty. I'd have to get up and paint to work it off. The only nights I did sleep at all were the nights we all slept on the sectional together. I knew I'd be better off to just ask everyone to do it every night since construction on the new bedroom had stopped while Casey was working at home.

I couldn't bring myself to ask. The nights we weren't all together were because Misty left to be alone with someone. Casey needed her a lot and Andre did too. Their job was much harder than mine was. My job was just to sit there and contribute whatever half useless idea popped into my head. Casey and Misty always told me my ideas were good, but I knew they were just being nice.

Today was my day off, so I didn't even have the shop to distract me. I didn't like leaving Misty, but she insisted I not lose money over her. I'd normally never miss the chance to take my granny to the salon. It meant a lot to her and I loved that woman. I was willing to miss it to protect Misty, but she practically kicked me out the house and made me go.

My granny was sharp and knew I was seeing someone. She'd been pressing for me to bring her over for Sunday dinner and I kept putting it off. Under most normal circumstances, my granny would have loved Misty, but she was like a hawk and she would have recognized her as one of the women at the salon when she caught me with my shirt off. She'd launch the fucking Spanish Inquisition at Misty until she believed her it wasn't her that asked me to take my shirt off, then she would shoot her dirty looks for the rest of dinner for checking me out.

I already knew Misty was going to have an uphill battle with my granny because of what happened at the salon. I was twenty-nine, tattooed, and built like a semi, but my granny still wanted to protect me from evil women who might want to hurt my feelings. She'd eventually get to know Misty and end up loving her like I did, but Misty didn't need the epic shade my granny would throw at her while she came to that conclusion.

I made my way to the kitchen before Andre got up. The only thing we were allowed to touch in his kitchen was the coffee machine and I needed black fuel. Misty also really liked her morning coffee and so did several other people in the house. I flipped the coffee machine on and almost regretted quitting smoking when I joined the military. A cigarette would certainly take the edge off.

I wasn't about to pick up that habit again. It was gross and I already knew Jake was a smoker. Misty hated it and he smoked in the house she grew up in. If my granny smelled it on me again, she'd whack me upside the head and I'd never hear the end of it. It would give me temporary relief right that minute, but it'd be hell trying to quit again and it was hard enough the first time.

I was surprised when Misty came into the kitchen without Casey. Andre wasn't even up yet. Everyone was getting up early now to look into Rook. I was just up earlier because I wasn't sleeping at all. As soon as I saw her, I jumped up to make her coffee the way she liked it. I felt her hand on my arm and stopped to look at her. As soon as I stopped, she gave me this huge hug. Even fresh out of bed, she smelled amazing. Like some sort of baked goods.

"Aiden, I don't think you slept last night. Grab your coffee and come back to your room with me."

"The investigation—"

"Andre, Casey, and Gareth will handle it when they wake up. I've been helping Casey with his injuries and I haven't noticed you not sleeping. We need to fix that."

She grabbed my hand and started dragging me back to my room. I tried to protest. Casey needed her more than I did and we needed to be worried about Rook. "Rook—"

"Let's not talk about Rook today," she ordered. She set our coffee cups on the nightstand and pulled me into bed. She pulled my head down to her breasts and she started playing with my long hair.

It felt strange being held like this by Misty. I was the tallest out of all of my friends at six foot five. I dwarfed Misty by over a foot, but she was holding me like a child. I had to admit, it also felt really fucking good.

"Aiden, do you frequently have trouble sleeping or does it have something to do with me?"

"It's not you, it's this Rook thing," I sighed, snuggling my face into her soft chest while her fingers played with my hair.

"Rook wouldn't even be a thing in this house if it weren't for me. Do you regret talking to me at the salon? I brought this mess into all of your lives and Casey wouldn't be injured if it wasn't for me," she said softly.

I craned my head up at her and met her gray eyes. She'd been trying to help us with Rook and help all of us with our various issues, but did she really think we would be better off without her?

"You aren't thinking of running again, are you?" I asked, burying my face in her neck and squeezing her waist. If she did, I'd never stop looking for her. Her hands went back to my hair. She loved playing with my hair and I loved the way it felt.

"I know every single reason I should just disappear one night while all of you are sleeping. I know it would break my heart to do it. I also know if I left, Casey would put himself in danger dropping his investigation on Rook trying to find me. I put you all in danger agreeing to stay. I was the one that brought you all to Rook's attention."

"No, Misty, that's not true. We wouldn't have even

noticed Rook's queen if she hadn't tried to unsuccessfully hack Andre. Gareth went overboard with those properties and the trust. Gareth has this thing he calls *justice hacking*. He sees a lot of shit going out with his client. If he sees something he doesn't like, let's just say he finds something embarrassing on that person and they end up with their careers ruined or in jail. He took it too far with Rook. I don't think you were even on Rook's radar until the raid on Serena and Gareth took his money and property."

"No, he knew of me through Jake. If Jake fucked up with everything he did trying to get my money, why did he help him escape?"

"I would imagine he has plans to do the same for Dillion. If your whole game plan involved crooks and corrupt cops, would you trust them not to turn on you?"

"I suppose you're right. Jake would turn him in if they promised him protection and no jail time. I don't think Jake has given up and my mother is still out there somewhere."

"Rook doesn't strike me as someone who deals with mistakes kindly. I don't think Jake is with Serena like Casey thinks. I think Jake is somewhere being punished. I know Rook says he's coming for you, but he won't give Jake the satisfaction of being the one who takes you. I think Rook knows if he sends Jake, you'll probably make him permanently crap through a tube like he's pissing in a bag."

Misty giggled. "Aiden? Don't tell Casey or the others what I told you about thinking this is my fault. Casey blames himself too much and it's not his fault. I can't tell him it's mine or he'd blame himself even more. You aren't looking into Rook, so I can talk about these things with you."

"I feel pretty useless, Misty. I brought you here and I can't do a thing to help protect you against him."

"Yes, you can, Aiden. You can make me forget Rook and Jake. Casey, Andre, and Gareth only talk about Rook and finding him. I can't help being afraid sometimes about what Rook's plans are when he does make his move. I know you think you can't do anything with Rook, but why can't what you do help distract me from Rook? I need some time out of my day that is Rook free."

"I thought you were doing that playing strip chess with Andre?" I immediately regretted saying that as soon as it came out of my mouth. I wasn't going to admit to Misty I was jealous Andre could play a game with her that she enjoyed playing with her father, even if they were doing it in a naughty way now.

"No," she sighed, resting her cheek on my head. "Andre wants me to play chess with him so he can study the game better. I was the one that suggested strip chess so it could be something other than a way to catch Rook. It's fun and I love playing with him, but it's just another Rook thing."

"So, you need me to get your mind off Rook?" I could do that. I thought I was the odd man out with this, but Misty had her own ideas about how I could help. If she needed to be distracted from thinking about Rook, that was something I could do. I slipped my hand up her top and cupped one of her perky breasts. She wasn't wearing a bra and I felt myself getting hard.

"Do you think you can finally sleep now? Take a nap maybe?"

I rolled her nipple between my fingers. "With you in my bed with no bra on after you've been playing with my hair?"

Misty laughed. "Okay, I see I'm going to have to exhaust you first."

"Why do you always smell so good? It makes me want to eat you up."

"Do you want an answer to that?" she gasped as I went to her collarbone.

"Yes, because I want to buy you a lifetime supply of it."

"It's a shop in Paris that does custom scents. I told them what I wanted and they made it just for me. They ship me an entire line. Perfume, shampoo, body wash, lotion. My ex hated it. You really like it?"

"I really hate your ex, Misty. He sounds like a total prude who didn't enjoy anything in life and didn't know what he had when you were with him. I'm glad you dumped him. I love your custom scent. It's warm and comforting, just like you," I said, planting kisses all over her neck.

"When was the last time you slept, Aiden?"

I groaned and doubled my efforts on her neck. I would have pinky swore to sleep every night when I realized I was this close to her with no bra on. I still had my hand up her shirt playing with her nipple. Misty was normally very responsive and I would have done anything to get her to do that now instead of worrying about me.

I knew I had her when she arched her back after I

bit down on her earlobe. "Kiss me, Aiden. I feel like I haven't kissed you in forever."

It hadn't been that long, but it seemed like ages for me too. She had been mostly staying with Casey while he recovered. We'd had a few play sessions on the sectional without him, but everyone was so worried about Casey and Rook, everyone was stressing in their own ways.

I claimed Misty's mouth, caressing her tongue with mine. She wrapped her legs around my waist when I rolled on top of her. I ground my erection into her belly. There was so much I wanted to do to her, but she wanted to be kissed right now. I would always do what Misty wanted or what she said she needed. Sometimes I asked her to do things, but only if I thought she would be comfortable with it. I never wanted to do anything to upset her.

"Aiden," she moaned. "What do you need right now, Aiden?"

"You. Only you. I only want to please you."

"I need all of you, Aiden. I want you to take control. I feel like I've been neglecting you."

I wasn't angry with her like she seemed to think and I needed to show her that I wasn't upset with her. Between the four of us, I couldn't imagine how she was feeling when she had to choose who to spend her night with when we weren't all together.

"Stand up," I said, tapping her shoulder.

I know she wanted me to take control, but I wasn't into rough sex or some of the things the others did to her when we were together. I had no idea straight-laced Casey was into spanking or anal sex. Hell, I had no idea adorable Misty was into ass play either. I was too worried about hurting her to ever go there with her, even if she seemed to like it. I'd have to think long and hard about it if she ever asked me to as well.

When she was standing in front of me, I gently pulled her top off and got a better view of those beautiful breasts. I couldn't have painted them better if I was doing an original painting. They were high and perky with pink nipples. They should be immortalized in a painting and hung in a museum they were that perfect.

I pulled her to me and took one in my mouth, gently licking and sucking. I did like touching her ass and massaged it with my hands. All those years of ballet lessons she told us about gave her a perfectly rounded ass and toned thighs. She was perfect and that was why I wanted to paint her all the time.

Misty's head fell back and she grasped my shoulders to steady herself. I felt her breathing pick up and she was moaning my name the way I loved. I knew she wanted me to take her little shorts off, but she also told me to do whatever I wanted. And what I wanted was to worship her body now that I had her alone. Even her breast in my mouth and her ass in my hands was enough for me, but she was mine today.

It still didn't mean my dick was straining against my shorts and desperate for attention. I growled and pulled her closer, gently biting her nipple.

"Aiden, please," she begged.

Only when I decided I'd given those perfect breasts enough attention did I gingerly peel her shorts off. I kissed her flat stomach, tonguing her belly button, before I let her back on the bed. I decided her legs needed attention next. Misty was short, but well proportioned. I knew a little about dance from going to see performances and she had the perfect little ballerina body.

I kissed my way down her thighs to her feet. I knew she'd been stressed about Rook, so I stopped there and started to massage her feet.

She moaned again. "Oh, god, Aiden. I don't know if I want you to keep doing that or fuck me."

"I'm not fucking you today. I'm going to make sweet love to you until you can't speak and want to take a nap with me."

"I'm ready for whatever you want to do to me."

We'd all been under a lot of stress and as much as I wanted to slide into Misty, I also wanted to make her laugh. I tickled the bottom of her foot and I'll be damned if she didn't moan like it was erotic instead of me trying to make her laugh.

"I think the bottom of my foot is like my collarbone, Aiden. That turns me on instead of tickling."

I kissed my way back up to her stomach, proud to have found one of her sweet spots instead of just hearing about it. Convinced I'd kissed every inch of her body, I parted her thighs. She was wet and waiting for me. Misty smelled of baked goods and tasted of vanilla. I gently teased her clit with my tongue.

"Aiden, I thought I was making you feel better today," she groaned.

"You are, love. Every cry, every moan, makes me feel much better."

"I love you, Aiden. I really do."

That was all I needed to hear to lick her a little

harder. Her hands found my long hair and she was pressing my face into her pussy. I easily slid my fingers inside her. Listening to her cry my name and tasting her was having a huge effect on my dick. I wanted her so badly, but I also didn't want to rush this.

I knew Misty's signals and noises. I only sped up when I could tell she needed me to. I could tell she was close, so I worked her fast and hard. When I felt her come hard on my fingers, I slowed my tongue down to drag out her orgasm. When she was finally still, I kissed my way up to her mouth. I was aching to take her.

"Are you ready for round two, love?"

"Yes, Aiden. Make love to me," she said, caressing my cheek and looking deeply in my eyes.

Sliding into her was like sliding into heaven. I had to stop and just enjoy her around my cock. She begged me to kiss her again. I stroked her cheeks with my thumbs and nibbled on her bottom lip. I lazily slid in and out of her, relishing how good it felt to be inside her. She kept her eyes open and those intense gray eyes never left mine. She was with me the entire way.

Her hands were clutching my back and her long, red nails dug into my flesh when I picked up the pace. I'd hardly gotten started with her when I felt her come. Her eyes still never left mine and her head snapped up to claim my lips. I slowed my rhythm just a little before picking it back up again.

I was still taking my sweet time, delaying my orgasm, but I started thrusting in earnest when she clawed my back again. "Aiden, I love you!" she cried.

I wanted to make her come again. With me this time. We were both sweating because I had been stroking her with my cock for so long. I could feel my balls tightening and knew I was close. Misty clearly knew my signs too and knew I was holding back.

"Let go, Aiden!"

I felt her pussy clamp down on my dick as she came again. She came harder than any woman I knew. It set me off and I roughly thrust into her as I spilled my seed. Misty was howling and clawing my back. I had my face buried in her neck grunting as I came. I needed that orgasm. I was about to pass out and sleep for days.

I moved to get off her and she wrapped her legs around me. "Sleep inside me."

I couldn't think of a better way to sleep."

3

I didn't just take a nap. I slept all day, all through the night, and didn't wake up until the next morning. I was a little disappointed Misty wasn't with me when I woke up, but I knew she probably had to eat. I was so tired, I didn't even feel her get out of bed. I hoped we got to do that again soon.

Breakfast and my friends were waiting for me when I woke up. I felt like I hadn't eaten in a month. In addition to not sleeping, my appetite had gone to shit. Andre had a huge feast for me and Misty made my coffee the way I liked it. Today appeared to be *baby Aiden* day. Everyone was trying to talk me up. Misty. It had to be.

"Aiden, since Misty is staying with me while I recover, why don't you just join us in my room," Casey suggested. "I've got a huge king that'll fit the three of us."

I eyed Casey. I was almost certain Misty asked him to ask me that. Out of all of us, I was sure Casey liked this arrangement the least. On the rare occasion he didn't dump someone first, Casey was super possessive in his relationships and ended up driving people away. He didn't look upset at asking me this. Casey was a horrible liar and wouldn't be able to fake it if he wasn't okay with me in there. If it had really pissed him off, he would be in his bedroom punching things and Misty would either be in there trying to calm him down or asking me herself.

He saw me staring at him and his blue eyes softened. "Misty didn't ask for this. We've been so wrapped up with Rook, none of us noticed you not taking care of yourself except Misty. We only realized when you passed out for two days. You always do this to yourself when you are stressed. You stay up for a week, then you get some sort of flu and can't get out of bed for days. I asked Misty if she would mind you sleeping with us since you seem to actually go to sleep if she's there. We both need Misty right now and I can't keep hogging her."

I know I must have sat there with my mouth wide open. Casey was the most against this arrangement at first. He agreed to it, but I could tell he didn't like it. He didn't seem totally on board until that night on the sectional when Misty asked him to take her ass while I was buried in her pussy. Casey didn't just get possessive over women. As kids, he hated sharing his toys too. Misty seemed to be having quite the effect on him.

"Thanks, man," I said when I was finally able to speak.

Andre and Gareth both offered their beds if they were alone with Misty too. I wasn't quite sure I understood. I knew we all enjoyed playing together on the sectional, but even I cherished my alone time with Misty. They were all giving it up just because I was having trouble sleeping. Casey was right. I did do this every time I was worried about something. The guys probably knew this perfectly well too. I realized how much I appreciated my friends right then and there. We'd always had each other's backs and now they wanted to help me since Misty was there to tell us it was okay.

"Can you get today off work?" Misty asked, rubbing my shoulder. I'd slept through my day off and I felt much better.

"I can't. Badger is off today and I can't close the shop because I have a long session on a back piece I'm working on that I can't cancel. He always schedules on Wednesday because it's a slow day."

"I forgot. Sasha and I have been talking and texting since we met. She and Badger have a picnic at the zoo planned then she tells me she plans on fucking him ragged when they get home."

I knew Sasha and Misty were going to be fast friends when I suggested inviting them over. Sasha didn't take much, like Misty didn't, and she was fiercely loyal to those she cared about. Sasha talked about Misty when she was in the shop too. She wanted to take her out for drinks and all I could tell her was that it wasn't safe for Misty yet.

"Sasha desperately wants to get at your nose with her needles," I said, grinning.

"Yes, I know. My lips too. She wants to put a jewel in my nose and she keeps talking about something called snakebites for my lips. She wants to pierce both, dress me in leather, and take me on a bar tour."

Misty looked a little sad. I knew she visited New Orleans before during Mardi Gras during college, but she hadn't been taken on a proper tour. We couldn't. We didn't know what she was hiding from before, then we needed to protect her from Jake, now we had Rook to worry about. She hadn't seen the zoo, the parks, we hadn't taken her on any riverboat rides, nothing.

"This mess with Rook will eventually be over," I said, even though I wasn't quite sure about that. "We'll all show you the best things about New Orleans and you'll be safe to go out with Sasha."

"I know, Aiden. You all keep me plenty entertained in the compound. Are you sure you're rested enough to go to work?"

I was the only one leaving to go to work now, but I had a lot invested in this backpiece and when it was done, Owen agreed to let me enter it in a contest.

"Yes. I'm excited to get more work done on that piece. And it's getting towards that time where I'm going to have to start gathering shit for tax returns. My least favorite part of owning a business."

Misty's eye lit up and I had no idea why. "Let me help you, Aiden. I can't work because of Rook and have money so that I don't really have to. There's not much I can do as far as the Rook investigation. I worked for a major acquisitions firm in LA before I ran and I majored in business. Why don't you and Badger focus on making art and let me focus on the business side? I can totally do your taxes and do them in a way that you get money back."

I scratched my beard. That would take a huge load off both me and Badger. Sasha too as she tried to go through the huge mess of bookkeeping we had for taxes during tax season. "Are you sure? It's a huge mess."

Misty grinned. "Not when I'm done with it. If you'll let me, I can promote your work and get you into more galleries too."

"So, you'll be my business manager?"

"Yes, and the only payment I want is kisses."

I totally loved that girl. I didn't have to go to the shop until one. I was shocked when I got a call I needed to get there now. Someone had vandalized the shop. Casey had to grab Misty because she wanted to come with me, but Gareth wanted to come. Andre had security cameras set up everywhere and he knew more about them than I did.

I was a hot mess as we drove to the shop. The long drive seemed to take forever this time as I wondered what the hell went on while I was sleeping. The shop was in a good part of town and we always saw good people. We did turn down people sometimes, but we always did it in a way that they weren't mad when they left.

I wracked my brains trying to remember if we pissed anyone off lately and I came up with nothing. We hadn't turned anyone away in a few weeks now. Gareth squealed into the parking space in front of the shop and I just stopped when I got out the car. Gareth came to a halt when he came up beside me.

"That son of a bitch!" he yelled when he saw the same thing I did. There was a chess pawn spray painted on the front door of my shop.

There were two cops waiting for us. One of them looked grim and the other looked a little pleased with himself. I had to resist punching the one that looked happy.

"Casey not with you?" he sneered.

Gareth put his hand on my chest. "I think you know Casey is injured," he snapped.

"What's the damage inside?" I gulped.

Badger and Sasha pulled up right then and they were both furious. "What the fuck?" Badger yelled, running his fingers through his bleached hair.

"Pieces of shit," Sasha growled.

"We might as well go in and see what the damage is," I said, knowing I didn't want to see it.

It was worse than I could have imagined. All my thermal imaging equipment had been smashed to pieces. Custom tattoo chairs were ripped to shreds. The smell of solvent assaulted my nose. We spent a lot of money on custom epoxied floors. They were totally ruined. My eyes didn't want to look up. I had this feeling of dread in my stomach about what they could have done to the walls. Before Badger and I opened our doors, we spent days designing and painting murals on the wall like I had done in my bedroom. I took two walls and Badger took two.

Knowing it couldn't wait, I let my eyes go up. Red paint was splashed on every surface and there was a huge, crudely painted chess piece from floor to ceiling on every wall. I knew enough from talking to Misty to identify them. There were two rooks and two queens adorning my walls now.

"Shit!" I heard Badger yell. Not knowing what could

possibly be worse, I walked over to our supply closet to see what it was. It was worse.

We didn't use autoclaves in our shop. We used brand new, disposable needles and wrapped our tattoo guns in plastic when we worked. They'd gotten to our entire supply. Everything was ripped open from its wrap and on the floor. It was totally unusable. We didn't have a single needle to tattoo with except for what we had at home.

"Check your station," I told Badger, stalking out to mine.

Not only did I not have a single working needle in the shop, but all of my high-end ink was also now on the floor or my chair. I started yanking the drawers of my station open. All my ink was gone and I couldn't find my tattoo gun at all. Badger was across the room screaming his was destroyed, but mine was gone. A trophy, perhaps?

I didn't understand this huge pissing match that had taken place in my shop. They might as well have put us out of business. This was going to shut us down for a long time to get it back the way it was and I didn't think my insurance was going to cover everything that had been ruined here today.

I felt Gareth come up behind me. I'd totally forgotten about him. He'd set up the same security cameras here as we had at the house and must have been reviewing the footage from his phone.

"It was Serena and someone who looked like an older man. They were both wearing masks. Serena had a cat mask on and the man was wearing a jackal on his face. The man's mask covered his entire head, but I recognized Serena's haircut from the photo Casey showed me."

"So, the Queen and which chess piece fucked up my shop? Why my shop?"

"Come home and talk, Aiden. Everyone has a surprise for you and I think I figured out why Serena is called the Queen from that video. I'll come back and help you clean all this up tomorrow."

I managed to convince Badger and Sasha to just leave it until tomorrow. If Serena and Rook wanted to hurt Casey or Misty by trashing my shop, all they did was ruin my livelihood and a dream I'd had since I got out the military. Talking wasn't going to cheer me up. Sex wouldn't either. I wanted to pull a Casey and just lock myself in my bedroom and punch things.

I knew everyone would get pissed at me, but this was an attack on my life and art. I'd been so motivated to paint lately and now I didn't think I could even look at a canvas without feeling like vomiting.

4

I was practically begging Gareth in the car to prevent anyone from coming after me when I went to my bedroom after we got home. I legitimately thought I was going to break into tears at any given minute and I didn't want anyone to see me like that, especially Misty. Beating me up when I got off work or kidnapping me and torturing me like they wanted to do to Misty would have made sense to me. Attacking my art didn't. I just didn't understand it. If this was to hurt me and not Casey, job well done.

I had to pass the living room to get to my bedroom and everyone was sitting there. Gareth had been furiously texting the entire time I was trying to get him to be my wingman and make everyone give me space. No one talked at first when I got in.

"We got a surprise for you. It's waiting with Misty in your bedroom. And, Aiden? I already know you're going to ask and the answer is yes," Casey said mysteriously.

I didn't even think I could get it up right now if Misty was waiting naked in my bed promising to act out any kinky fantasy I could think of. I wondered if she would understand if I asked to be alone. It wasn't that I was trying to push her away, I just needed it.

Misty wasn't naked when I opened my door. She was laying next to a strange lump. Before I could even open my mouth, there was this huge gray blur as the lump flew off the bed and knocked me flat on my ass. There was something wet on my face and I realized I was looking into the eyes of a beautiful adult blue-nosed pit bull. I didn't know if it was a girl or a boy, but it still had its natural, floppy ears instead of being cropped. It'd just met me, but it was laying on my chest licking my face.

I had no idea why there was a dog here. I'd always wanted one, but Andre had a no pet rule in his house.

"King, come!" Misty called. The dog ran back to Misty and hopped right into my bed. Misty stroked its head and patted the bed. Maybe their surprise might make this shit day better.

"Casey told me all about how you would bring stray animals home. *You* told me if you could, you would take an adult, hard to adopt, dog from a kill shelter. Andre said the only reason he has his no pet rule was that he thought if he let you bring one home, you'd bring all of them home. This is King. He's five years old and had just been surrendered by his family to a kill shelter. Since he's a pit bull, they intended to list him as available for twenty-four hours, then euthanize him just because of his breed. I picked him out to save his life and I thought you would like him. He just so happens to be named after a chess piece. Maybe he'll bring us luck in this investigation."

"How did you—how did you know I find pit bulls majestic and misunderstood? You just adopted my perfect dog and saved his life."

"He's gorgeous and sweet, isn't he? I was never allowed to have a pet growing up. When I ran when I was sixteen, one of the men who lived by the cabin I was hiding out in had a pit. I was so scared of that dog at first, but it was like she wanted to prove to me she was harmless. I loved that dog. I love pits and think they are misunderstood too. I knew she was perfect for you because I've seen some of your sketches. You always draw pit bulls when you draw dogs."

Casey's statement still confused me. "What was Casey talking about when he said he knew I would ask and the answer was yes?"

Misty giggled. "It was actually *his* idea if you can believe it. Casey invited you to sleep with us so you would actually sleep and now you have a dog. Casey said as long as the dog doesn't get creepy when we are having sex, he can sleep in the bed with us."

King was lying on his back with his tongue hanging out while Misty and I scratched his belly. I shouldn't have doubted Misty or my friends. This was one of the best surprises after a shit sandwich I had ever gotten. Life was starting to make a little more sense again. My shop was trashed, but I had Misty and three best friends who cared about me. I could rebuild the shop. I was being an idiot for thinking I'd rather be jumped in an alley than my art trashed. Things could be replaced. People couldn't.

"*Casey* seriously suggested I sleep with the two of you, *then* suggested my dog could come? Misty, are you fibbing with me and all of this is your idea?"

"No, Aiden, it was really Casey. He shows this hard shell to everyone, but when he goes off alone, he beats himself up over everything. He blames himself for Jake and Dillion taking me and I'm sure he thinks what happened at your shop is his fault. It's mine too. Rook and Serena wouldn't have trashed your shop if we hadn't disrupted their board. They can't get inside the house, so they trashed your shop because it was the only thing they could get to."

"I don't blame any of you, but this pisses me off. I want to find a way to bring them down. Gareth said he thought he figured out why Serena was called The Queen of the board? Should we go out and talk?"

"Gareth texted us. Are you sure you want to know? Some of the stuff that went down in your shop got a little gross."

It couldn't be any worse than what I already saw. "I need to know so I can help you bring them down."

"We think Rook himself was in your shop. Serena is called the Queen because they are lovers. She got paint all over her back when they fucked against the wall when they were done trashing the place. It seemed like they got off on it."

Misty looked at me like I had a second head and King rolled over and cocked his head at me when I cracked up laughing. I laughed so hard I had tears pouring down my face and my stomach was starting to hurt. That was just the jewel on top of the wreckage I saw at my shop. Some old fart and his girlfriend who trolled sugar daddy sites befouled it further fucking all over the place. If the health board found out someone fucked in my shop, even without the wreckage, they would have shut us down.

"Aiden?" Misty said, touching my arm. She was looking at me like she was worried this had driven me totally mad.

"I'm sorry, Misty. That's just the cherry on top of everything they did at my shop."

"Did you want to talk about it?"

I didn't. I wanted to forget what I saw at my shop and what apparently happened after they were done destroying all my hard work and property. "Why did this big guy's parent drop him off at a kill shelter?" I asked, scratching King's head.

"They just found out they were having a baby. They didn't even try to find a no-kill shelter or another home. They drove home from their appointment confirming it, picked him up, and just dumped him at the kill shelter. If they had a pit bull for five years, I'm sure they knew what would happen to him there. Stupid reason to get rid of a dog anyway. Like you can't have both. Ed's pit grew up with his four sons."

"You really are my dream woman, Misty."

"Do you want to show me or did you want to take King out to play? Andre and Casey also stopped at the pet store and got toys. He loves fetch with the squeaky ball."

"We're all sleeping in Casey's room tonight, right?" She nodded. I didn't want to be alone anymore. I was never into much kink until our nights on the sectional and I didn't peg Casey for being into it at all. I wanted some kink tonight to get my mind off my shop.

"Let's go throw the ball and play for the rest of the afternoon. I'll show you when we're with Casey."

5

Misty really did pick out the perfect dog for me. I'd wanted a pit bull since I was ten and found one roaming the street. My granny refused to let me keep her, like all the strays I brought home. She'd let them stay until I found them a home, but after that, they were gone. I'd asked for a dog several times growing up. My mother had been allergic, so I couldn't have pets. After my granny started raising me, she thought the same thing Andre apparently did. If she said yes to one, she'd have a million animals running around her house.

King was all pit. Stocky and muscular with a blocky head. He was also a huge goofball that just wanted to play fetch and get belly rubs. Misty and I got tired of throwing the ball well before King got tired of fetching it. My arm was starting to get sore, but I kept throwing that squeaky ball because watching him bound after it like an eighty-pound puppy just made me smile every single time the ball flew out my hand.

Andre and Casey had just grabbed a bag of food at the pet store and it wasn't good enough for my new dog. I read the bag and it was full of by-products and filler. No, tomorrow, I was going to get him a huge bag of premium, grain free food so he would stay muscular and have a nice, shiny coat. Worrying about what to feed him got my mind off the shop.

I was sure Andre was going to say something when Misty and I came out the backyard to eat with everyone and King bounded in with me and sat between Misty and me at the breakfast bar. I was sure I was about to get a lecture on no dogs where we ate. Andre took his kitchen as seriously as I took my shop. I would have made sure King wasn't there if he asked.

Andre shocked the shit out of me. "We grabbed that food at the store so he would have something to eat when he got home, but I was researching dog food while Misty was picking him out. Apparently, the raw diet is really good for dogs. So, I'm going to start cooking for King so he eats just as good as the rest of the house."

Who was this and what had he done with Andre? Preparing raw for my dog? I wanted to do that for King, but the kitchen was off limits for me and I wasn't going to press it because Andre was already letting me keep a dog in his house.

"Oh, stop giving me that look, Aiden," Andre said, grinning at me. "I fell in love with that damned dog too when we were picking him up. I think we all did. He looks like he's capable of tearing your throat out, but he's kind of a huge baby, isn't he?"

"Thank you. All of you. This really cheered me up

after I saw my shop. I intended to just ignore everyone when I got home. I had no idea any of you were going to do this, but I needed it."

"That's what we're here for, man. And Casey and I looked at the footage from your shop. We have a little more info on Rook now."

"Are you sure it was Rook? Wouldn't he send a knight or a pawn for vandalism?" I asked. It didn't make sense for Rook to come personally trash my shop. It just seemed like he was this shadow that had an army of chess pieces to do his dirty work.

"Think about it. Rook must have been playing this game since at least the late nineties. He's been teaching that online course since then and it's probably been going on longer, just harder for him to recruit. No one has ever suspected him or his players before. We are closer to him than he wants us to be and he's going to get sloppy," Casey said. "I think he trashed your shop with Serena because he's frustrated he can't get to me. He's trying to make me careless and acting in anger. I'm even angrier than I was before, but he was the one careless this time."

"What could you have possibly learned from the security cameras? He was wearing a mask."

"Tons," Gareth said with a mouth full of food. "He's definitely a cop or a retired cop. Just moves like one. He's about six feet tall and left handed. Serena did most of the trashing and he was the one that painted all the chess pieces on your walls and the front door. I'd bet money he took a bullet to his left shoulder at one point and it still hurts him."

"But you don't have his face or identity," I pointed out.

"No, but we know Serena is staying with him. She's still in the state. What we could tell from the video narrows my search down a little."

I didn't want to think about Rook anymore. He'd already taken too much from me and he was a constant danger to Misty and my friends. Misty said she needed me to distract her from the constant conversations about Rook in the house. I needed Misty and Casey to do the same for me tonight.

"Casey, can we go back to your room?" I asked.

He just gave me a curt nod and I was starting to think he really wasn't okay with me sleeping in there with him. Misty disappeared to take a shower since she smelled like dog and said she felt filthy from wrestling with King in the grass. I loved that about her. She was this little rich girl with a trust fund, but she never talked about money and she was totally willing to get down on King's level to wrestle with him. He had her pinned on her back slobbering all over her face and she was shrieking with laughter.

Casey just slipped out of his clothes and laid on the bed in his shorts. I left all my clothes on and stared at him.

"If you aren't okay with this, I can go back to my room."

Casey looked surprised. "Why do you think that? I was the one who suggested it. I'm not going to lie, Aiden. Sometimes, I see you as my rival since you met her first and worry one day she will pick you or Andre over me. But I know I'm probably just being stupid. I know I'm hogging her since I got injured. I know what happens when you don't sleep. Can you not see that I know you need Misty too so I'm trying to make this work?"

"After Iris—"

"Don't *ever* compare Misty to Iris. This is different. *I'm* different now or at least I'm trying to be. I don't want to do anything to drive Misty away and you're one of my best friends. I know you need her right now because you're not sleeping. *I* need her right now because I'm having nightmares about Rook taking her. She's going to try to leave again if we're all pulling her in one direction. This is for all of us."

I never thought I'd hear anything like that out of Casey's mouth. Actually admitting he was having nightmares and needing someone, talking about his feelings. He just never did that before. He normally just locked himself in his bedroom and worked out until he got over whatever was bothering him.

"Casey, have I been a bad friend? Should we have been dragging you out your bedroom and making you talk instead of just letting you do what we thought you needed?"

Casey just chuckled. "No. I probably would have punched any one of you and you can't exactly do the things Misty does to calm me down."

I grinned at him and was about to speak, but I heard the door to the bathroom open. I knew Misty was coming out and she didn't need to hear us talking about all that. My mouth totally dropped open and my dick got hard when she walked out of the bathroom dripping wet without a stitch of clothing on. The smell of her custom scent hit my nose and my dick was actually hurting it got even harder. I watched a drop of water roll off her pert nipple like it was in slow motion.

I heard Casey groan from the bed, but I couldn't peel my eyes off the water nymph in front of me. She put her hands on her hips and raised an eyebrow at me. "I see you still have your clothes on."

I immediately went to pull my shirt off and she stopped me. She said she wanted to try something. I knew everything we had been doing with her was new to her, even that first day alone in my bedroom. I knew her ex didn't bother taking care of her in bed. She seemed to have *a lot* of things she wanted to try in bed and we were all eager to please her. I wondered what my little pinup girl had in store for me tonight.

"Aiden, I want you to dance for me again. I loved the dance you all did for me and I want Aiden to do it again. While Aiden is giving me a show, I'm going to give him one. Casey, take your shorts off and lay with your head at the foot of the bed."

I saw her grab the remote to Casey's stereo. If she wanted another dance, I'd shake my ass and strip just for her. The problem was, Casey's taste in music mostly lay in depraved screaming and I didn't think Misty knew that. I didn't think I could make Casey's taste in music sexy no matter how I danced. It sounded like someone was torturing a chicken.

I was surprised when Misty hit play and some sort of erotic music came on. She must have gotten to his stereo system like she had the one in the living. I had no idea what kind of show she had planned for me, so I started slowly swaying and lifted my shirt to show her my abs.

I finally realized what kind of show she intended when she slid down Casey's dick and her eyes never left mine. She bit her lip and was slowly grinding herself into Casey's cock. She ordered him to play with her breasts and he immediately did what she asked. I desperately wanted to get my pants off because my dick was straining against them so hard, it hurt, but I wanted to give her a good show.

Misty rode Casey harder with every item of clothing I removed. Her eyes never left me and I loved the way she was hungrily checking out my body. I was down to my boxer briefs and Misty was riding Casey even harder. He was practically growling underneath her like he wanted her to ride him even harder, but he was restraining himself for her show.

I pulled my shorts off slowly and my dick breathed a sigh of relief. The music was done and I was totally naked. I fisted my dick and started pumping it as Misty was now practically bouncing on Casey's cock. I stroked myself slowly because I didn't want to blow my load yet and this was fucking hot.

Misty raked her manicured nails down Casey's chest and I guess he couldn't stand it anymore. He sat up and practically devoured her neck, growling at her to go faster. Misty gave him exactly what he wanted and was soon howling like a cat as her orgasm ripped through her. Casey wasn't far behind her. They collapsed together in a heap on the bed and I was just standing there with my dick in my hands feeling like a third wheel.

Once Misty recovered, she got off the bed and walked over to me with bedroom eyes. She ran a fingernail down my chest and started stroking the tip of my dick with her finger.

"I can't decide if I want to get on my knees and have you fuck my mouth or if I want you to take me from behind. What do you want?" she purred.

I couldn't fuck her mouth without choking her and that wasn't my favorite thing to watch on porn either. Misty on her hands and knees was the more appealing option. I'd never done that with her before. I swooped her up and carried her to Casey's bed. She must have already known what I had chosen because she got on her hands and knees and started wriggling that perfect ass at me.

"Let go tonight, Aiden. I'm not breakable."

I wrestled her onto her back. My dick was aching for her, but I wanted to kiss her first. She was still wet, both from the shower and from sweating from that little show she put on for me. I could feel her slick against my body and I think even after everything we'd done, I'd never been this turned on with her before. Even kissing her right now felt like our very first kiss.

Misty and I were never rough with each other, but I found it sent jolts straight down my spine when she dug her fingernails into my back and I felt her teeth on my bottom lip. I wanted to nibble on those perfect nipples. Misty was writhing and begging for more before I'd hardly even gotten started.

"I want Aiden behind me and Casey in my mouth," she gasped.

After that show she had given me, I was ready to

burst and I would have agreed to anything she wanted. I yanked her up to her hands and knees like she was a doll. Casey was already erect and ready for her again. He groaned when she took him deep into her throat.

I was behind her and slid into her slick pussy slowly, enjoying every inch as I entered her. I had her much deeper this way and I was buried in her as deep as I could go. I started slow, but between Casey's grunts and Misty's cries, I needed my release.

I had no idea what came over me. Maybe it was the shop getting destroyed, maybe it was after watching Misty with the others, I knew she sometimes loved it that way, but I started really pounding her from behind. I'd never taken a woman that hard before. It just wasn't me. Misty seemed to love her. She was crying all over Casey's dick and her pussy was fluttering all around my dick like she was doing that on purpose.

I reached my hand between her legs and started circling her clit with my fingers while I was fucking her from behind. I'd hardly touched her when I felt her pussy on my dick like a clamp and she was practically screaming all over Casey's dick. I didn't even give her time to recover. I slammed my dick in her even harder and my fingers sped up on her clit.

I knew I wasn't going to last much longer. Casey was done and leaning back on the pillow watching me like a contented cat. I totally blew my load when Misty started slamming her ass against me and came all over my dick again. I collapsed over her back and nuzzled her neck.

"You're a little minx, you know that?"

"Do you think you can sleep now?" she asked innocently. She just had to clamp her pussy down on me right when she said that.

I didn't think it was possible after I came that hard, but I felt myself stir again.

"Later," I growled in her ear. "I'm not done with you yet."

6

I was in the middle of the most peaceful sleep I think I'd ever had when the dreams started. Misty kept Casey and I entertained for hours. I fell asleep exhausted cuddled into Misty with the sweet smell of her custom perfume tickling my nose and King sleeping on my feet. I had been dreaming of Misty in a few years, close with my granny, and we were all so happy.

I was leaning in to kiss her in the middle of Andre's garden in the compound as King chased his tail around our feet when she morphed into a man with a jackal head and the scene changed to my shop. I could see him and Serena trashing the place, but I was powerless to stop it. They couldn't hear me and my hand went straight through them when I went to grab their arms.

I bolted awake panting and sweating. I knew now why they hit my shop. I knew why I was their target like I knew the back of my hand. I needed to warn Badger not to go anywhere near the shop. I grabbed my cell phone off the nightstand and bolted into the bathroom. Misty's hand grazed my back as she called my name in a worried tone. Misty was safe for now, but Badger wasn't.

"Call a meeting in the living room," I called over my shoulder. I could hear rustling behind me. I must have woken Casey because I could hear him trying to calm Misty while they got dressed.

It was five in the morning and Badger was going to be passed out. He always waited for Sasha to get home and had dinner waiting for her. She stayed up late writing her thesis and he stayed up with her reading. I was going to get an earful from both of them and I would have to tell them about Rook and the truth about why our shop was targeted. I just kept hitting Badger on speed dial hoping he didn't put his phone on silent.

"Aiden, what the fuck?" he mumbled.

"Someone had better be dying!" Sasha shrieked.

"Badger, you can't go anywhere near the shop until it's safe. I'll figure out something on getting it cleaned up and running again."

"No go, man. I raised a huge shit show to get an adjuster out tomorrow at noon. They wanted to wait two weeks to send someone out."

"Put the phone on speaker so Sasha can hear. Do you remember when we were asking all those questions about Queen? Queen is actually a cop named Serena and she's apparently the lover of another corrupt cop with a huge network. Casey tried to bust Serena and she left a bomb for him. Serena was one of the people who trashed our shop. If you're going to be there tomorrow with the adjuster, you need to find a way to do it and check for bombs."

"Queen was a cop? I want in on whatever you're doing to bring her down," Badger growled. "She harassed my girl and trashed our shop."

"I want in too," Sasha said. "And I've got a network of people at work who may have the info you don't."

"Both of you should stay as far away from this as possible. The shop was an attack on me and my friends."

"Aiden, don't be stupid," Sasha snapped. "Don't you think if she's a cop, she stalked the place out first and knew I was dating Badger? It wouldn't be too much of a stretch to link her bust to me. She wanted me really badly for her club and she knew I hated her. I didn't try to hide it. It wouldn't be hard for her to guess if Casey was looking into strippers, you'd talk to me and I'd mention Queen. She works pretty hard to make herself distinctive. Casey would know it was her as soon as I described her."

"Yet another reason for Badger to be far away from the shop tomorrow. If Serena also wants to hurt you, she wouldn't hesitate to kill Badger. We can't go back to the shop until we know it's safe."

"Please, Badger, just do what he says," Sasha pleaded. "I know you're worried about money, but you can be a bouncer at the club until the shop is safe."

I knew Badger wasn't hurting for money, but I knew why he told Sasha that. He was saving all the money he had to take her to Las Vegas and propose on one of the gondolas in the canals. He had the whole thing planned out, but he wanted to save up enough for the proposal, the wedding, and the honeymoon. Sasha always joked she wanted to get married by an Elvis impersonator, so intended to get married in Las Vegas then immediately take her to Greece, which she talked about wanting to go when she got her Ph.D.

Our shop getting trashed was ruining Badger's plans to give his girl her dream wedding when she finally graduated. And Sasha could be in danger too.

"Maybe Sasha should lay low for a while too. Both of you."

Sasha just laughed. "No, we're both safe at the club. The owner is bigger than you are, but goes by Peanut. If I tell Peanut Queen is a corrupt cop and have evidence what was going on at *The Defiant Palace,* she'll be roughly escorted off the block and security will keep a keen eye out for her. We're safe at my job."

"Just be careful, okay?" I said, disconnecting.

Everyone was in a state by the time I got to the living room. Misty flew at me and practically tackled me with a hug. "What is it, Aiden? You just bolted out of bed and ran to the bathroom with your phone."

I led her over to the couch and she jumped straight into my lap when I sat down because she thought I was upset about something. I wasn't feeling helpless and unable to help this time. This time, I knew what Rook's game was and it was going to be me helping and keeping my friends safe. I started twirling a piece of her hair around my finger and stroked her back.

"It came to me while I was sleeping. I'd been trying to figure out since I saw those chess pieces painting on my trashed shop why Rook would personally come fuck up the place. Oddly, it was the gross sex against the wall that gave me the answer. They weren't getting off on the destruction. They were celebrating what they *thought* was their victory."

"Explain, Aiden," Casey said, leaning forward with his elbows on his knees.

Misty stroked my beard. "If you have the answer, Aiden, tell us. The only reason we can think of that he targeted you was to piss us off."

My ego, which I normally kept in check, but was practically non-existent since this whole Rook thing started swelling. I could actually keep my friends safe and give insight to Rook this time. I was finally a contributing member of the team aside from just moral support.

"Think about it. They had to know there would be some sort of security cameras up and Serena only covered her face with that cat mask. We would be able to tell it was her. The attack on my shop was bait. They can't get to us in the house, but if my shop was ruined and you knew Serena did it, half of you would be there looking for clues and the other half would be there to help me clean the place up. They trashed my shop to get us out in the open, in one place, to pick us off. It'll either be another bomb or there will be pawns and knights there to disable us and bring us somewhere Serena and Rook can have their revenge."

"That's—that's brilliant!" Casey yelled. "Gareth and I would have gone so I could see if I could get Rook's fingerprints and Gareth found anything I missed. Misty and Andre would have gone to help you clean up. We all would have done it without hesitation too."

"I know that and so does Rook. Rook knows you,

Casey, or he's got pawns that know everything about us here," I said.

"That's…almost impossible," Casey said, rubbing his face. "There are a lot of people that know I have roommates and that we worked together with Jake. They know the people in this house are responsible for Dillion getting arrested, but they don't know how close we all are or that we'd do anything for each other."

"It wouldn't be impossible to find out we all grew up on the same street and have attended the same school together since kindergarten. It also wouldn't be hard to find out we enlisted together too. Four kids that grew up together, enlisted together, and all live together at twenty-nine? It's not a huge leap to make the assumption we'd all be there for Aiden when his shop was trashed," Andre said.

"Can we get bomb-sniffing dogs in there?" Misty asked. "If you can clear it for bombs, I'd like to hire a cleaning and construction crew to get Aiden's shop back up to where it was. For Badger too. Sasha says he's always complaining about money. This is probably a huge blow for him, being out of work."

I didn't tell Misty Badger's big secret because it wasn't the time. "Misty, insurance can handle it." I didn't want her spending her money on me.

"Didn't you ask me to be your business manager? Let me handle insurance, cleanup, and construction. I'll have the place ready for you when all this Rook shit is done."

"On one promise. You use insurance money and not your own money on the shop. And if it gets to be too much, tell me and I'll take over."

Misty wriggled so that she was straddling my lap and she stroked my face. "I actually *need* this, Aiden. I was working sixty-hour work weeks when my mother called and said she wanted my help leaving Jake. I know I have money and don't need to and you are all doing a wonderful job keeping me entertained, but I miss working. I like to work and I get the feeling you'd rather skip the business part of arts and just make it. Can't we be partners? I do what I enjoy so you can do what you love."

I nipped at the tip of her nose. "You mean you actually like insurance policies, the health board, balancing the books, and the IRS?"

"Probably as much as you like painting."

"So, it's settled then," Casey said, totally snapping me out of how turned on I was right then. "I'll call Leo to get a squad at the shop to clear it for bombs and Misty will handle this getting the shop back in order."

"What if they bugged the shop so they know when we get there?" I asked, focusing on the task at hand instead of the beautiful woman sitting right on my dick. "I don't get the feeling they'd be doing a stakeout on the street waiting for us. They aren't stupid."

"No, they aren't and I'm such an idiot. I should have checked for that when I was there with you," Gareth said, getting angry. "I was too busy reviewing the security footage, but they could have planted something while their backs were to the cameras and they were destroying the chairs or those carts you use to store your supplies."

"Gareth, don't be mad at yourself," Misty said. "With everything going on that day, you identified Serena and we got a little more information on Rook. There wasn't enough time to rip the chairs apart for bugs with everything going on."

"We *have* to make time for everything. We can't miss any detail. If Aiden hadn't been the only one of us with a lick of sense, we all would have been at the shop later in the day to either get blown up or kidnapped!"

Misty was off my lap in seconds and had Gareth in a hug. "But Aiden did see what Rook's plans were and we are safe now. Since we know, we can come up with our own plan."

"I'm too fucking pissed to come up with any ideas. That fucker ruined Aiden's shop just to get us all together. You've never been there, Misty. The whole shop looks like Aiden's bedroom. Someone could have taken photos of the shop walls and hung them in a magazine. Now they are covered in red paint and chess pieces that looked like they were drawn by a drunk fourth grader. And those savages had some pretty disgusting sex against the wall," Gareth ranted. "I had to turn the volume off at that part."

I hadn't seen the video yet, but apparently, everyone else in the house had. "Did they say anything we could use? Did Casey recognize Rook's voice?"

I had no idea why we were all sitting around doing nothing if Casey could identify him now. "If we have Rook's voice, don't we have Rook now?" I asked, running my fingers through my long hair. I had no idea why Gareth was so pissed if we had everything except Rook's face.

"We have the noises Rook makes during sex," Gareth snapped. "He grunts like a stuck pig and Serena wails like a fucking hyena. He never said a word while he was painting your walls. Serena laughs like a damned hyena too. That was the only sound from those two while they were trashing your shop. We still don't have enough to identify him."

"Mother fucker," I swore. Based on what we had right now, even if Misty did get the insurance claim through, the shop cleaned out, and new equipment ordered, it may be forever before it was safe for me and Badger to set foot in there again.

"Everyone is tense and rightly so," Andre said. "Did you want me to cook? I'll even make steak for breakfast."

I nearly got up and punched Gareth when he roughly grabbed Misty and threw her on the sectional, but she started laughing and seemed to like it.

"I want Misty, then steak," Gareth growled.

I saw Misty bite his ear pretty hard. "Are you in a sharing mood, Gareth? I think everyone is tense."

Gareth was already attacking her collarbone. "May I have your ass this time, Misty? I haven't before."

"You only ever had to ask, Gareth."

Gareth was being rough as he tugged her top off. I wondered if I was the only one in the house that *didn't* want her ass because I was worried about hurting her. Gareth had her flat on her back and he didn't look like he wanted to share. We all just kind of hung back, ready to leave, if he needed her right now.

"Is everyone going to get naked?" he asked, nibbling on her breasts.

I stripped, not sure what he wanted. This was Gareth's show this time. He gruffly asked all of us to get over there and show our girl some attention. I was the furthest away, so I got there last. Casey and Andre already each had a nipple in their teeth, so I drew her head in my lap and stroked her hair while exploring her mouth with my tongue.

Misty was having trouble staying still as Gareth furiously lapped at her pussy with his tongue. Her hands found Casey and Andre's cocks and she started jerking them off. They both removed her hands. She didn't know why and was begging to touch them. That was when I realized what this was. Misty was going to have a hell of a day today.

Gareth brought her right to the brink, then withdrew his tongue. "Gareth, you always tease me," she moaned.

"I want to watch you play with your pussy, Misty," Gareth said. He positioned himself and eased into her ass.

I was transfixed as I watch Gareth pounding her ass while she fingered herself and Casey and Andre gave her nipples attention. I knew what Gareth was doing. I stayed with her head in my lap until it was my turn. Gareth, Casey, and Andre all made love to her while the rest of us worshipped her body. It felt awesome to give my girl that much attention. She'd been running herself ragged trying to be there for us. We needed to be doing this for her.

She was panting and sweating when it was my turn. We all told her we loved her before we entered her and when we finished. I was the last. Misty needed to be told we loved her as much as possible, especially with everything she told me in private about Rook. I didn't want her to try to leave again because she thought she was a burden to us. Not after what happened to my shop. She needed to be told we loved her as much as possible.

"I love you, Misty," I said, lazily stroking her clit with my thumb.

Her gray eyes met mine and I could tell how much she needed this. There was relief, happiness there. "I love you too, Aiden." She said that to all of us both times we said it to her. There was no falsehood there. She really did love all of us as much as we loved her.

Andre had been here just before me and had taken my place with her head in his lap. He was playing with her hair and stroking her cheeks. I lifted her hips like she was breakable and placed them on my knees. She wrapped her legs around my hips as I slid into her. She was slick and warm after my three friends already pumped their loads into her.

I held her hips up with one hand and massaged her clit with the other as I slowly thrust myself in and out. Watching Casey and Gareth pay attention to those perfect breasts and the look of bliss on her face was just egging me on. I'd hardly gotten started with her when I felt that familiar flutter around my dick as she came. She cried out my name and those intense gray eyes never left mine.

I locked my eyes onto hers and picked up my thrusts once she had recovered. She liked to look into my eyes when I was making love to her. It always seemed like she was looking directly into my soul. I groaned when she bit her lip to stifle a cry. She looked so adorable. I started working her faster with my dick and thumb. She screamed my name when I felt her come again.

That just set me off. My orgasm ripped through me like a tornado. I yelled her name right back as I thrust sharply into her. It felt like I was never going to stop coming.

"I love you, Misty," I roared as my dick finally stopped twitching. Casey and Aiden moved as I set her hips down and collapsed on top of her.

She started petting my beard. She seemed to love my beard. "All of you are so amazing. I needed this. I hope you did too."

"Misty, *we* need to be showing *you* how much we love you, not the other way around," Gareth said. "We need to be worshiping the ground you walk on in addition to protecting you."

Everyone murmured their agreement. We could all see Misty was about to cry at what Gareth said, so Andre changed the subject.

"I also need to feed you. All of you snuggle down and I'll cook."

7

ndre liked to give Casey and Gareth a hard time for being uncultured savages for wanting to live off burgers and steak instead of the gourmet meals he always cooked. It was something they gave each other a hard time about, but Andre prepared their favorite meals at least once a week and Casey and Gareth really did like and appreciate the food Andre cooked. It was just one of those things we liked to rib each other about.

I'd become a vegetarian when I was thirteen after watching this video online. My granny flipped at first because I was still the runt of our group then. She was worried I was going to die of starvation, but she soon realized I was going to stick to my guns. She got online and ordered every single cookbook she could find and even started eating vegetarian with me because she was cooking huge, elaborate meals every night. My granny had always supported me no matter what I wanted to do.

I hit my growth spurt at fifteen and seemed to never stop growing. I hit six foot five at sixteen and got more interested in working out like my friends. Andre got bullied like I did, but he started working out and bulking up at fourteen. I was the last of my friends to grow and start working out in Casey's garage with everyone. I started out the runt of the group, but now I was the biggest out of all my friends.

Every time Andre made steak or burgers for Casey and Gareth, he always made me one of my favorite meal too. There were plenty of my granny's recipes I loved, but Andre had taken his recipe for Bang Bang Shrimp and turned it into a tofu dish. While I was snuggling on the couch, I was pretty sure that was what he was making.

When Andre called us in to eat, I was right, but I also had no idea why he put a bowl of Bang Bang Tofu and Sesame Miso Zucchini Noodles in front of Misty. Casey and Andre were looking at her like they wanted to take her straight to bed when she ate that steak with them. They hadn't had any conversation with each other before Andre disappeared.

Misty saw me staring at her bowl. "I asked Andre during our chess games to prepare me some of your favorite foods too. I'm afraid I don't know what this is."

I let Andre take over and explain the modified tofu recipe and noodles. Misty hadn't asked about my diet yet, but she did as she was eating my favorite food with me. I explained the video I watched and the support from my granny. Misty had just asked me if she was ever going to get to meet her again when my cell phone rang. It was my granny and I swear, that woman had to be psychic or have some sort of third eye.

"Aiden?" she yelled as soon as I picked up. "I heard about your shop. Why didn't you call me? Are you hurt? Who did this? Are you in trouble?"

She always fired off a million questions when she was worried and hardly took a breath to give me a chance to answer. I had to wait until she stopped to take in air.

"Granny, I'm fine. It just happened yesterday and I haven't had a chance to call yet. No one was there when it happened and I'm not hurt. Casey thinks he knows who did it. I've got a new business manager who is going to be handling everything with the vandalism and she's going to be getting my work into galleries too," I said, winking at Misty.

"She?" Granny shrieked. "It's that girlfriend you've been avoiding talking about! You can't let some woman control your art, Aiden. And your poor granny hasn't even met her yet to know if she's a good fit for you."

I groaned inwardly. I might as well just rip the Band-Aid off. "You have met her, Granny. I met her at the salon. She was the girl I asked you to talk to. The small one with the gray eyes getting her hair dyed."

"The Jezebel that asked you to take your shirt off?"

"Misty wasn't the one that asked me to take my shirt off. It was Camille. Misty was just there."

"Hrmph. Remind me not to tip Camille again when she does your toes."

"She always does your toes?" Misty demanded. She sounded a little jealous. Misty was trying not to be seen checking me out when Camille got my shirt off, but

Camille looked like she was about to go for my fly. Now, I had both women in my life mad at me I took my shirt off in the middle of the salon.

"I heard that," Granny said. "Sounds like she's got some sense. I've never liked the way Camille looked at you. When can I meet her? I need to get to know her better if she's going to be in your life. And I need to have a little girl chat with her to make sure she doesn't break my little puppy's heart."

I was probably the color of an eggplant. *Little Puppy* had been her nickname for me for the longest time. She still called me that when I either did something good or she was worried about me. I couldn't look at Misty. She probably thought I was some coddled granny's boy. I couldn't speak. I was worried my voice would break or I would say something I'd regret.

"I'm not sure what to call you, but we'd be happy for you to come eat dinner with us so you can meet me and see I mean Aiden no harm," Misty said.

My granny sniffed. "Finally, someone is talking sense. Young lady, you may call me Granny if you're good enough for my grandson. If not, you will call me Mrs. Fournier as I unhook your claws from Aiden's life."

"Yes, Ma'am."

"At least you have manners, unlike Aiden's last girlfriend. I'll be over tonight at six. Tell Andre nothing spicy tonight. My indigestion is acting up."

I was mortified as I hung up. The guys all knew how my grandmother was, but Misty didn't. I felt her touch my arm again, but I didn't look up.

"Aiden, it'll be okay. We'll all put on a show like I'm

just with you so she doesn't suspect what's really going on. I'll do my best to charm her."

I finally looked up. Misty wasn't looking at me like she thought I was an overgrown child dependent on his granny. She looked deep into my eyes like she understood what I was going through.

"It's sweet your grandmother worries for you, Aiden. My grandparents passed when I was a baby so I never met them. You know what happened with my mother. I think it's amazing you have someone in your life that loves you that much."

I rubbed my face in my hands. That was easy for her to say. She hadn't been on the receiving end of one of my granny's verbal assaults because she thought someone wasn't good enough for her grandson.

"You heard what she said about my ex having no manners? She dumped me right after I brought her home to meet my granny."

Misty just laughed and kissed my cheek. "Good. She had no manners anyway and if she hadn't dumped you, you wouldn't have asked me to stay here at the salon. What did she do that your grandmother said she had no manners?"

"She really didn't," Andre said, wrinkling his nose. "We never said anything, but we didn't like her either. We didn't like her giving you orders or when she tried to order us around."

I finally laughed. "Now that I think about it, neither did I. If my granny hadn't gotten to her, she was already talking about having my name tattooed on her and she wanted me to put her name on my body too."

Misty giggled. "The name curse you told me about?"

"Gets you every time. Badger and I refuse to do it. She wanted me to break our rules and do it together after dating her two weeks."

"You're such a romantic, Aiden. Why did you take her home to meet your grandmother if you didn't really like her?"

"I have no idea, Misty. I guess I was lonely and confused. I met her at a bar near the shop and it seemed like a good idea at the time. When I saw you at the salon, it was nothing like when I saw her at the bar and went to talk to her. She was at the bar waiting for someone to pick her up. I could tell you were hiding something as soon as you walked in. Your eyes were darting across the room looking for any threat. It just made me want to put you at ease and protect you."

Casey cleared his throat. "We need to talk about the task at hand instead of Aiden's exes. We need to clear the shop so Misty can get an adjuster in there. I don't think it's safe for Aiden or Badger to go back to work until we've caught Rook and Serena."

"Insurance claims take time. I was researching it while Aiden went to the shop. Louisiana has thirty days to pay property damage once a claim is initiated unless there are extenuating circumstances. I would say Aiden's shop falls under that category. It may take a while before we see a payout, especially when I cancel the adjuster for bomb-sniffing dogs."

"After Serena's little present at her house, it's going to take a while to get a team out at Aiden's shop. I can give you a little info that may ease your mind. The bomb at Serena's house was triggered to go off when they broke the door down. Serena would have had to have gone back to the shop to plant the bomb if that was what their plan is. It could be they just wanted us all in one place because they want us alive," Casey said.

"Like any of us would go down without a fight," Gareth snorted.

"I think they know that, Gareth. If they sent a knight or a pawn, they'd have access to riot gear and tear gas," Casey pointed out. "I don't want anyone going anywhere near Aiden's shop until Rook is caught."

veryone knew to dress sharply when my granny came over. Even I dressed up. Misty came into my bedroom while I was doing up my tie. She had a modest black dress on and had played up her gray eyes the way I liked. She came over to help me with my tie. I had no idea where she'd learned to do a tie and asked.

"My father taught me. He always hoped I'd fall in love with a nice boy in college and do his tie before he took me to expensive dates on the town."

I pulled her into a hug and kissed the top of her head. "When all this is over, I'll take you on the most expensive date I can afford and you can do my tie."

She rubbed her face into my chest. "I'd prefer fun over expensive, Aiden."

I tickled her waist. "So, you'd go paintballing with me?"

"Yes, and I'd totally shoot you right in the chest," she

teased, swatting at my hands. "Is this dress okay for your grandmother or should I change?"

"She'll love it, but she's going to want to know how you afforded it and if I bought it for you."

"Is it okay to tell her I have a trust fund and don't intend to take your money?"

"Yeah, I actually think you should. I may have had an ex I blew a lot of money on when I got out the service. She was just using me for gifts. It'll ease her mind."

"Aiden, hearing about your exes makes me jealous," Misty growled.

I kissed her forehead. "Well, my granny is going to mention all of them and you'll probably get on her good side if you bad mouth them a little with her."

My granny always got everywhere she was going thirty minutes early. She was sitting on the rearranged sectional when I walked out with Misty on my arm. My granny stood and gave me a huge hug and just glared at Misty.

"Mrs. Fournier, it's so nice to meet the woman who raised Aiden and cares for him so much," Misty said. Misty actually reached over and hugged my granny instead of shaking her hand.

My granny pulled away and eyed her suspiciously, but I could tell she was softening towards Misty. "Did Aiden buy you that dress?"

"No, Ma'am. When my father passed away, I inherited a large sum of money. I can buy my own things without demanding anything from Aiden. My father was a businessman and I went to school for the same thing. When Aiden mentioned doing his taxes always frustrated him, I offered to take over the business side of his shop and art. Numbers make me happy. That way, I'm helping Aiden and doing what makes me happy and Aiden can just concentrate on his art."

My granny sniffed. I could tell she was trying to think up something nasty to say and just couldn't. She wanted to dislike Misty and was finding it hard. "Were you close with your father?"

"Yes, Ma'am. I idolized my father. It was very hard when we got the news he died in a car crash. My mother remarried a monster way too soon after his death."

"And do you take after your mother or your father, Misty?" Granny demanded.

"I don't think I got anything from my mother at all. I look exactly like my father and I was always closer to him. My grandparents died when I was a baby, so if my mother had died with my father, I would have had no one to do what you did for Aiden. You raised a sensitive, caring man all by yourself. Aiden is one of the good ones and I wouldn't do anything to hurt him."

I watched all the ice melt away from my granny as Misty's flattery finally got to her. My granny actually smiled at her the way she smiled at me and she had *never* done that with any of my girlfriends she had met.

"I think, my dear, you may call me Granny like these four boys do. Do you really think you can help Aiden with this vandalism and take away the burden of all the things he dislikes when it comes to making his art?"

"I do. And I want you to meet someone. I got Aiden a present while he was at the shop viewing the extent of the damage. I'll be right back."

Misty disappeared and I knew she was getting King.

My granny leaned over to whisper in my ear. "I like this one. Don't do something against everything I've taught you and mess this up."

"Never, Granny. This one is special."

I didn't think it was possible, but my granny looked at Misty with a new respect when King came bounding out and started sniffing her hands. She scratched behind his ear.

"You did this for Aiden? He's always wanted a pit bull."

"I know. I talked it out with Andre, Casey, and Gareth and got permission. I picked him out and we went to adopt him. Andre is cooking for him."

My granny looked at Andre like she was shocked. "I thought you hated dogs? You wouldn't let my Aiden get one when he moved in."

Andre winked at my granny. I always thought my granny had a secret crush on Andre now that we were older with his sweet words and delicious cooking. I think he knew too because he always flirted with her and it creeped me out.

"I actually do like dogs, but I thought if I let him get one, he'd turn this place into an animal shelter. I have a full menu planned for the dogs. Are you ready to eat? I made your favorites. Shrimp and Corn Bisque and stuffed Mirlitons. I also made fresh strawberry cheese-cake for dessert."

Granny giggled and let Andre take her arm to lead her to the kitchen. "When are you going to move in with me and be my personal chef, Andre?"

Gross. I already knew my granny had a secret boyfriend. Not so secret anymore. She wrecked her car a few years ago and had to call me. He was with her and that's when I found out she was dating. I was actually glad for her, but she was horribly embarrassed I'd found out. It was a widower from her church and she made him leave before I got there. We never talked about him because I didn't think she wanted to talk to me about it.

I started asking to drive her places more after that accident and that was when we started doing our salon dates every Friday. I'd drive her to get her hair done, then I'd take her to lunch. I had no idea if she was still seeing her friend from church or if they broke up and that was why she always seemed to hit on Andre when she was around him. The idea of my eighty-four-year-old granny hitting on my twenty-nine-year-old best friend creeped me out, but they both seemed to enjoy the banter, so I never said anything to either of them.

"You know I love cooking for you, Granny. You should come eat with us more often so I can cook for you and see that beautiful face."

My granny giggled like a school girl. Dinner was super awkward. I wanted to slide under the table and die. My granny alternated between mentally undressing Andre and openly flirting with him to telling Misty every single embarrassing story from my childhood. I thought she would just want to rip on my exes if she decided she liked Misty, but oh, no. Misty had to hear about the time I got sick in kindergarten and she had to pick me up because I had crapped my pants.

It seemed like every mortifying thing that had ever happened to me was flashing before my eyes the more wine my granny drank. I kept my face buried in my food and just wished for this night to end. I felt Misty squeeze my leg under the table. I dragged my eyes up to meet hers and her gray eyes were sparkling.

"Aiden sounds like he was an adorable child."

"Andre, thank you for the meal and the conversation," Granny said, putting her napkin on the table. "Misty, you have been wonderful and I think you would be amazing for Aiden. I'm afraid I've drunk a bit too much wine and should get home."

"Granny, let me drive you," I said, jumping to my feet. "You shouldn't drive drunk."

"You're right, Aiden. You're such a good boy. I suppose I was just celebrating good company and you finding Misty and drank a bit much."

The drive back to her house was long. I never thought I'd never hear these words pass her lips about a girl I was into, but she spent half the car ride gushing about Misty and how pretty she was. She spent the second half passed out in her seat snoring. When I finally got to her house, she looked so peaceful, I didn't have the heart to wake her.

I had keys to her house, so I unlocked the front door and tried to get her out the front seat of my car without waking her. She never stirred as I carried her to her bedroom and put her to bed.

She may have embarrassed the hell out of me tonight, but that's what southern grannies were for and I loved the hell out that woman. I tucked her in and left her peacefully sleeping.

9

It was still early when I got home, but Misty met me at the front door. Earlier that day, before my granny arrived, Casey tried to arrange for a squad to clear my shop for bombs and Misty called the insurance company. We still didn't know who we could trust at Casey's precinct, so he was only talking to Bishop and Leo, who he swore he could trust. If Casey thought he could trust them, then who was I to say otherwise? I knew nothing about either of them.

Misty met me at the door with King and pulled me to my bedroom. "Come snuggle with me, Aiden."

I dove into bed and pulled her to my chest. My hand lazily stroked her arm while her fingers made circles on my chest. "Your grandmother is sweet. I think she's very proud of you."

"She didn't have to give a play by play of all the embarrassing moments of my life," I admitted.

"It was sweet, Aiden. Even when something was

embarrassing for you, she was proud of you. Did she get to bed okay? She was a little drunk."

I laughed. "She was totally shit faced. My granny is a lightweight when it comes to drinking."

"Was it just me, or does she have a thing for Andre?" Misty asked, laughing with me.

I told Misty my story about my granny's secret boyfriend and that she always hit on Andre. Misty couldn't stop giggling. "Your grandmother is a little scandalous. And I think Andre was eating it up she was flirting with him all night."

"I know! It's gross. My granny is like *his* granny. She practically raised all of us and he talks to her like she's our age."

"Knowing Andre, he does that for her. He wants her to feel young and beautiful, so he flirts with her like she's his age."

"You know, I never thought of it like that. I thought he was doing it for *his* ego, not hers. You're right. I should probably stop getting mad at him when he does it. He's doing it to make her feel good and I think she's a little lonely since I moved out."

"I do like your grandmother, Aiden. She's quite a spitfire and she does care about you a lot. You should invite her to dinner more often if she's lonely. I think she'll love seeing you happy, she'll eat good food, and Andre will talk her up."

"You're right. I call her every day and we have our weekly date at the salon, but she's eighty-four. She's healthy as a horse, but I need to be spending as much time with her as possible. For both of us."

"I think she'd like that. I know the boys will have to

pretend while she's here, but I want to be close to your grandmother, Aiden. I know how much she means to you. I'd like to meet Casey's mother and Gareth's parents too. Andre doesn't have anyone left, like me."

"You have us, Misty. Casey's mom is a huge mama bear, but she'll love you. You wouldn't believe it from how Gareth acts, but his parents must be the two most boring people on the planet. They get up, go to work, they have a set menu they eat during the week, they watch the evening news, then they are in bed at nine. They never go out and they never deviate from their routine. That's probably why Gareth is so spontaneous and acts on his whims. He can be a little reckless sometimes."

"Don't blame Gareth for your shop, Aiden. Casey and I played a part in that too."

"I'm not blaming any of you for my shop. I'm putting the blame right where it belongs. On Rook and Serena's shoulders."

"You saved our asses, Aiden. I would have walked into your shop without hesitation, either with the adjuster or with everyone to help clean up. You don't have a single mean bone in your body, but you were able to think like Rook and save us."

"I wouldn't say that. I've been cruel to people before. I've hurt people. I was very angry when I got out the military and I lashed out at everyone, even my friends."

"And are you still angry, Aiden?" she said softly, playing with my beard.

"I started meditating and doing yoga. My anger passed, but it's peeking its way back in with all this Rook stuff. My shop, the fact that I can't hunt for him like Casey, Andre, and Gareth are doing. I don't want to be that person again, but I feel it creeping up on me."

Misty jumped out of my arms and seemed excited. "You do yoga, Aiden? I love yoga! I got my certification in college and taught a yoga class twice a week back in California. We should do yoga together!"

Doing yoga with Misty's soothing voice would calm the raging beast that was threatening to come out. That was a horrible time for me. I was drinking too much and lashing out at everyone. I was smoking two packs of cigarettes a day and I was just using women for my own pleasure. When I looked at myself back then, I hated it. I never wanted to be that man again.

Misty had her chess games with Andre. Yoga could just be our thing. But I wanted a little extra. "Naked yoga?" I suggested, cocking an eyebrow at her.

She laughed and swatted my chest. "That depends. Are you going to behave yourself when I'm in downward facing dog?"

She shrieked when I grabbed her and pulled her on top of me. "This is what I need. An intense, naked yoga session, meditation, then as soon as we're done, I intend to make love to you so hard you can't speak."

Misty buried her face in my neck and bit my neck. "Well, if that's what you need, who am I to say no? I'll enjoy the hell out of all of that too. Should we start now?"

"With you up against me like this? I can't do yoga with a raging erection. And I get one every time you touch me."

Misty kissed me deeply. "Let me take care of that for you then."

She had me out of my clothes in seconds. I groaned when her tongue swirled around the head of my cock. Her hands were massaging my balls. I kept impatiently thrusting my hips up. She was licking my entire shaft like a lollipop, but she wouldn't put it in her mouth and suck.

"Misty, are you *trying* to torture me?"

She looked up from my dick and gave me this devious little grin. "Something I learned from Gareth. Trust me. You'll like it. I did."

She went back to only just putting the head of my cock in her mouth. I couldn't help thrusting my hips up to get the whole thing down her throat. She would just pull away and give me this ethereal smile.

"Patience, Aiden," she would say as she pulled away.

My dick was stiff as an oak tree and desperate to be in her mouth. She finally gave me some relief when she started sucking on my balls and working my shaft with her hand. I felt like a parched man who had been stuck in the desert for days who had just been given water. She was only stroking me slowly, but her attention to my balls was enough.

"Oh, god, Misty, I need you."

My little angel took her mouth and hands completely away from me. There was so much pressure building up, I thought if she just looked at me, I'd explode. She climbed off the bed and pulled her dress and thong off. She couldn't wear a bra with that dress and I just admired her perfect body from the bed. My hand went to my cock to get a little relief from her teasing.

"Nope, Aiden," she said, gently removing my hand.

"Misty, you're killing me," I groaned.

She hovered over my cock and lowered herself on me painstakingly slowly. When I was finally buried deep inside her. She just sat there with this content look on her face.

"You have a massive cock, Aiden. Has anyone ever told you that?" she asked, opening her eyes.

I was wriggling under her trying to thrust into her. I was practically rabid for her. "It's nice to hear," I grunted. "What do you have planned now?"

"Are you questioning me?" she demanded, slowing grinding herself on my erection. I love it when she took charge.

"More like begging."

She dipped her head back and started making slow circles on my cock. Instead of begging or thrusting. I reached up and played with her nipples as she slowly rode me. Her head snapped up and she looked deep into my eyes again. She moaned my name and sped up. I rolled her nipples between my fingers as she started getting harder and faster.

"I love you, Aiden. I love your cock. I love everything about you," she gasped as I felt her come.

She fell forward on my chest and wrapped herself around me like a koala bear. "Give it to me how you want it, Aiden."

I wrapped my arms around her waist and thrust into her hard and fast. I realized what she had done when I felt my orgasm building. She had delayed it so that when it did come, it was going to be dangerously hard. When I finally did explode, I clutched her to me and yelled so loud, King started barking.

"Jesus, Misty. That was intense."

"Can I sleep like this?"

"Casey—"

"Casey said he would be up late working and didn't want to disturb us coming to bed. He said to just stay with one of the boys tonight."

"I'd love to sleep like this," I said kissing the top of her head.

10

I was blissfully asleep with Misty draped across me with my dick still partially inside her when someone started pounding on my bedroom door. Misty groaned and rubbed her face in my neck. Casey came storming in and threw my pants at me.

"Bishop is here to see you. If he's here in person, it's bad. Get dressed and get to the living room."

Misty and I dressed in a hurry. Bishop just cocked an eyebrow at us when Misty sat close to both me and Casey and held our hands. It was pretty obvious who she spent the night with and I'm pretty sure he thought she was with Casey. All the noise must have woken Andre and Gareth because they came stumbling into the living room cursing. They stopped when they saw Bishop and joined us on the sectional.

"Son, you're going to have to tell me what sort of gang shit you've gotten yourself involved in," Bishop said, eyeing me like I had done something wrong.

"Gang shit? My shop gets trashed and you're asking me if I brought it on myself?"

"The gang symbols painted on your shop match another crime scene for someone close to you. Now, quit dicking around and tell me what you've gotten yourself involved in."

"Crime scene for who?" I demanded, bile rising in my stomach. Had Serena gotten to Sasha and Badger? Were my friends dead because I suggested bringing them into this?

"Your grandmother," Bishop said softly. "It looked like they tried to rob her and she woke up. I'm sorry, son, but they shot her in the chest. She didn't make it. The same chess pieces in your shop were spray painted on one of her walls."

I stumbled to a potted plant and vomited. I dropped her off and came home to have sex. I should have made her stay here. I should have demanded she stay here until this whole Rook shit was done. She was dead because of me. She was a target because their plot with my shop didn't work. Misty tried to catch me just as I was about to hit the floor and went down with me.

I was weeping like I had when I was a child, but now I didn't have my granny here to soothe me. "It's my fault." That was all I could manage to say. Andre hauled me to my feet. I thought I heard Casey yelling at Bishop, but I wasn't hearing much of anything. Andre looked like he was dragging me back to my bedroom, but I stopped and marched back to the sectional. I wiped my eyes and glared at Bishop.

"Serena, from *your* precinct did this. We have her on camera trashing my shop. Why don't you do your fucking job and find her instead of coming in her blaming me for gang activity?"

Casey was furious. "I *told* you it was Serena that wrecked Aiden's shop. What the fuck are you up to, Bishop?"

Casey *never* said fuck. I'd never heard that word pass his lips. He was pissed and looked like he was on the verge of breaking down. My granny was just as much his as she was mine.

"Why would Serena trash Aiden's shop and try to stage a burglary gone wrong on his grandmother? Serena has probably left the country by now!" Bishop yelled.

All of a sudden, the room was full of the sounds of horrible laughing. That laugh would haunt me for the rest of my life. It was this wicked, evil laugh and when I followed the sound, it was to the television screen. It was coming from a woman in a cat mask ripping my tattoo chair open with a knife.

"You see, asshole? Serena! She's still in Louisiana!" Gareth yelled. "You should have been looking for her when Casey told you she was the one at Aiden's shop so she and her partner couldn't go murder Aiden's grandmother!"

"Who is the man with her?" Bishop asked.

I wondered if Casey was going to cop to Rook. Misty was shooting him a look like she didn't think he should. I know Casey saw Bishop like a father, but something must have been going on with Casey.

"Her partner, her lover. Who knows? They have sex up against the wall later in the video. It's pretty gross," Casey said through gritted teeth.

"So, you have no idea who this man is?" Bishop demanded.

"No, we don't. For all we know, he's the ringleader of all this. Now, Bishop, we just lost a member of our family, so I'm going to need you to get the fuck out our house so we can mourn," Casey yelled.

Bishop just threw up his hands and stalked out. I was still in shock. I was sitting on the sectional with my face buried in Misty's neck. I didn't think I would ever be okay again. My friends piled on the couch with me in a huge hug. We all just wept openly at the loss of my granny. It felt like there was a huge hole in my chest where my heart had been.

This was all my fault.

I moved around the house in a haze over the next few days. I had to deal with funeral arrangements and her will. I had no idea her wishes were to be cremated because she never talked about it with me. I also found out she didn't want a funeral, she wanted a party. She left me my childhood house in her will, but I didn't think I could stay in there without her. I had no idea what to do with it.

I had to leave the house several times. Misty always wanted to come and we always had to convince her to stay. Gareth stuck me in Kevlar and was my armed guard when we went out. Everyone wanted to be there, but they couldn't be. Most of us thought this happened to get us all together at the funeral to kill us. That didn't make me feel any better. My granny died for some stupid revenge against me and my friends.

I wasn't in a party mood, but I planned one. We thought it was best to hold it at the house and screen anyone who came in. I knew all her friends from church and extended family who would come. I wasn't even paying attention to what was happening at my shop, but I knew Misty was working on it in the background.

Casey still wasn't healed yet, but he insisted we all sleep on the sectional together. I knew that wasn't him being macho. He needed it just as much as I did. We were all reeling from the loss of my granny. Even Misty, who'd only met her twice was taking this hard. No one knew what to say to each other. We mostly just lay on the sectional in a heap not speaking.

It was Gareth that broke our silence. "I can't keep doing this. That fucker *murdered* Granny. I can't sit here and do nothing. We need to start the investigation back up again."

"Can't it wait until after the party, Gareth?" Misty asked.

"No," I said. "I want to find Serena and Rook just as much as Gareth does. I want to see them both fry. Do you think they'll crash the party?"

"No," Gareth said, bitterly laughing. "I think they were counting on a public funeral to either bomb or pick us off. They would have sullied Granny's funeral just like they murdered her. They deserve to die!"

"This is what they want," Misty said, getting up to pace. "They want us angry and careless. We have to be vigilant now more than ever."

"I agree," Andre said. "This is going to take some behind the scenes work. Casey, I need you to get me a list of everyone who fits the profile of the man in the video. I'm going to get into their computers and find out what they are hiding."

King hopped on the sectional with me. He seemed

to know I was in a foul mood and slept on the sectional with us on my feet. The guys didn't seem to mind. He flopped his blocky head on my lap and his gray eyes rolled up at me. His eyes were a deeper shade of gray than Misty's. I scratched him behind his ears and found it had a calming effect on me.

He had been whining at all the yelling and he needed to me calm him. I couldn't save my granny and I was half wondering if I could save Misty if it came to it. But I could help calm King right now. It would make me feel like I had some semblance of power right now.

"It's okay, boy," I said softly, scratching his neck.

Misty noticed he was upset and came to sit with us. She nestled into my chest and started stroking his head too. "I'm sorry we upset you, boy."

"I'm going to feel pretty useless when you start looking into Rook and Serena again," I admitted. "I already feel totally worthless for inviting my granny here and not insisting she stay here."

"Come on, Aiden. Let's go to the garden with King and let the boys do their thing."

King leapt off the sectional when Misty grabbed his squeaky ball and stuffed sloth from his toybox by the couch. Misty had been going crazy ordering him toys online. I have no idea where she found that sloth, but it was his favorite. He slept with it every night like this big, brutish baby. He trotted behind us as we went to the backyard.

Andre had a pretty ornate garden out there. Most of the sculptures were mine. Andre was always a big reader like me and that was part of why both of us got bullied so much in school. If he wasn't on a computer and I wasn't drawing, we were usually in the corner reading. I was into graphic novels and Andre had a thing for mythology and fantasy. When he asked me to do sculptures for his garden when he was having this place built, he wanted gods and goddesses from his stories and nymphs and fairies playing in the flowers.

Misty sighed and wrapped her arm around my waist when we got to the clearing King could play fetch in. "It's so peaceful out here. Sometimes, when we come out here with King, I can forget Jake and Rook."

"It's not taking the edge off my anger this time," I admitted. Normally coming out here with Misty and King calmed me too.

"It probably won't for a while. I was angry for the longest time after my father's car accident. I'm *still* angry Jake is still out there and he was the one who murdered him. I don't care about what he did to me. I want him to pay for what he did to my dad."

I was only a child when my parents died. I didn't really know how to process it then. It was just kind of like they were there one day, then they were gone and I was living with my granny. There wasn't much I remember about them. All of my good memories growing up revolved around my granny. She was the one who taught me to ride a bike, taught me to drive, took me to get my license, and thought every girl wasn't good enough for me.

I didn't have the mental capacity to deal with losing my parents because I wasn't old enough. I was twenty-nine now and I wasn't sure how I was supposed to deal with it now. I knew I had people around me who understood. Misty lost her father and just found out he was murdered. Andre watched his mother waste away to cancer.

I had people I loved here who understood what I was going through a little, but it wasn't Misty's fault her father was murdered and it was no one's fault Andre's mom got cancer. It was *my* fault my granny died. I could have slept at her place that night since she was drunk or I could have insisted she sleep it off at our place. I should have just told her I was in trouble and I needed her to stay at the compound with us. I didn't. I lied to her, then came home and had sex.

"Aiden?" Misty asked, snapping me out of my dark thoughts. "They have to be watching the compound to know about your grandmother. Maybe we can help with the investigation by looking at the security footage outside the gate. Did you see any cars on the road when you were bringing her home?"

"That's a fucking great idea, Misty. I want to see if someone followed me. There's plenty of places for a car to hide. Sorry, King, we're going back inside."

He was running back with the ball in his mouth. Apparently, Misty had been playing fetch while I was off in space. King was such a good boy and didn't whine on the way back in. Misty just had to shake his stuffed sloth and he trotted behind her happily. When we got back inside, everyone was sitting at their computers looking frustrated.

"I want to review the security footage outside the gate," I announced. They hadn't even looked up from their screens when we came in.

Casey looked up at me sadly. "You think they got to her because they followed you home?"

"It's the only thing I can think of so far."

Misty and I sat snuggled into the sectional reviewing the footage from the night I took my granny home. There was nothing. No car lights coming from the trees like we were followed. I was about to explode and trash the television.

Misty put her hand on my arm. "Maybe they were further down the road where there are no cameras."

"I have something!" Gareth yelled. "I got into the court system from when Granny was made Aiden's guardian. I tried to look into who accessed that record. Grant Winder accessed Aiden's records. He did it from his personal computer, but he's the only person who looked at those records, *and* he's a cop."

"Grant's not Rook," Casey sighed. "Another pawn or knight. Probably a pawn. Grant is straight out of academy and writing parking tickets. Like Serena, he should probably move to tech, but Rook has him there for a reason."

"Fuck!" I yelled. It seemed like we were never going to find Rook or Serena.

"Casey can bust Grant for Granny's murder. He's at least an accomplice," Gareth said.

"But who did he send the information to?" Casey asked. "Is there a trail leading to Rook on his computer?"

"Just Serena and nothing recent. It's the same email she was using on that Sugar Daddy dating site and they haven't emailed since she tried to blow Casey up. There's nothing here about what Grant was doing for Rook, just threatening emails from Serena to be more productive. They have to be communicating by burner phone."

"Any luck on that number that texted Casey?" Misty asked.

"No," Andre said. "It belongs to a thirty dollar pay as you go phone purchased at Walmart with no Wi-fi or GPS. It's registered to an alias, but he put the last name Rook on it."

"I'll call Leo," Casey said, gingerly getting up to make that phone call.

"What if I take away Rook's cushy adjunct job at that online school?" Gareth murmured.

"Gareth, don't," I said. "Let's avoid pissing him off until we have more information. He could go after Badger and Sasha next."

"We have something though, Aiden," Misty said, stroking my beard. "Grant could give us information on Rook and if he was the one that hurt Granny, he'll pay."

It didn't make me feel better at all.

12

The next day, we were all pacing and antsy. We had been sleeping on the sectional together since we got the news about Granny, but I don't think any of us slept that night. Casey wasn't even close to being cleared to go back to work, so Grant's arrest was in Leo's hands and none of us knew if we could trust him. I had no idea why, but Casey didn't even tell Bishop. The only person that knew Grant was being arrested was Leo and he was doing it at the office.

While Leo was questioning Grant, only then did he plan on bringing anyone in to search his house. This was the only safe plan Casey could think of that didn't involve bombs this time. We all knew Grant was supposed to report to duty at nine to do reports, then hit the street for duty. Leo was supposed to arrest him as soon as he got to his desk.

Casey asked for photos of the rook painted on the wall at my granny's house. We already knew it wasn't Rook at the house last night. Well, I knew and told the others. I could tell from the lines in the drawing that they were done by a different person. Whoever was at my granny's house seemed nervous and they had a shaky hand as they painted the rook on the wall. That wouldn't be Rook. He probably didn't get nervous over anything.

It seemed to take hours. Nine passed, then ten, and eleven before Leo finally called Casey. Casey put the phone on speaker.

"I'm almost fairly certain Grant was the one who killed her. They called me out while I was trying to question him. He's got an unregistered Ruger and a silencer at his house. They already determined it was a Ruger that shot your friend's grandmother. I'll bet ballistics matches this gun to the bullet they took out of her."

My hand tightened on my knee. He was talking about my granny like she was just some random corpse and not someone's family. Like she hadn't raised me and my three friends since we met in kindergarten.

"Has he said anything?" Casey asked.

"No. We tied him to the vandalism at the tattoo shop because of the graffiti but he refuses to say why he targeted your friend."

"Serena trashed the shop, Leo. We have her on video with an older man in a jackal mask. If you need more evidence, the chess pieces on the wall tie Grant to Serena."

"But it still doesn't link to Dillion, does it?" Leo asked. "I'm taking a break for lunch. Can you think of anything I can ask him?"

"Find out if he went to any type of online college," Misty said.

"Who the hell is that?" Leo demanded. "Why does she have access to our investigation?"

"You didn't meet Misty when she came in to give her statement. The link between Jake and Dillion is that they went to the same online college. It's a good idea, Leo. Maybe Serena and Grant went to the same college."

"It's a longshot. Grant is pleading the fifth to everything. He hasn't asked for a lawyer, but he's got this smug look on his face like he thinks he's going to get off."

"Where is Grant now?" I growled. "And before you ask, it was my granny he shot."

"He's in a holding cell. Holy shit! There are alarms going off everywhere. The power went out at the jail and the generators aren't kicking back on."

"Dillion," Casey said. "This is why Dillion took the fall. Someone is helping him out. Get off the phone and call the jail. Have them watch all exits!"

"We just can't win, can we?" I said, slumping in my seat. "Grant's in jail, but someone will just help him escape like they are Dillion right now."

"Yes, we can," Andre said, grinning at me. I knew whatever he said wasn't going to help me feel better. "Serena and Grant both went to ULL together. She was a senior when he was a sophomore. She had been a senior three years without showing any signs of graduating. Serena and Grant dropped out at the same time. They both took an online class as part of their studies. Care to guess who the adjunct professor was?"

"Are you shitting me?" Gareth yelled. "How did we not find that?"

"Different name this time. He goes by Drake Rook at this school. Same story. A retired cop with no headshot doing it for no pay."

"He can't be an active officer then, can he?" I asked. "He wouldn't have time to teach all those classes."

"Unless he has a desk job, but he would be foolish to do that from work," Casey said. He was rubbing his chin. He used to always be clean shaven, but now he had been sporting this five o'clock shadow since Rook started. I had no idea how much of that was Rook or Misty liked it.

"So, we still have nothing," I said, slumping in my seat.

"No, Aiden, we have the man that shot Granny," Misty said. "We can tell everyone at her party tomorrow that he's in jail. This is something we should celebrate. Finding Rook is going to take time, but we have one of his pawns now."

I didn't feel much like celebrating.

13

I wasn't in the mood to party. Misty and Andre planned the whole thing because I wanted nothing to do with it. Planning that party meant my granny wasn't coming back. I knew she wanted this to be a celebration, but how could I celebrate being the cause of her death? Misty and Andre went all out. The house was beautiful and they both cooked a ton of food. There were wine and booze free flowing since she said that was what she wanted.

Gareth was screening everyone who came in. So far, no one came in that shouldn't. It was all her salon and church friends. I didn't even realize Badger and Sasha had come until they sat right next to me on the sectional. Sasha hugged me and took my drink. Misty had been trying to do that all night. I was actually avoiding her and I knew I needed her right now.

"Honey, you look like shit and you stink of whiskey," Sasha said. "Why don't you take Misty and go back to your bedroom if you hate all this?"

I grabbed her hands and made her look me in the eyes. I hadn't called him about my granny, but it made the news. "Promise me the two of you will stay safe. Serena—Queen did this. Her and a bad man. I'm scared for you two. I'm sorry I didn't call you. I should have warned you. I can't do anything right."

"Hey, shit head," Sasha snapped. "This is not your fault. Serena is a psycho bitch. You weren't even responsible for her getting busted. She bombs sexy Casey and she hurt a helpless old lady. When Casey catches her, she's going to fry. And she's stupid enough to still be in Louisiana, so she *will* get caught."

"I could have warned my granny or—"

Sasha walloped me on the back of my head like my granny used to do. "Misty?" she yelled. "Get your hot ass over here."

I could feel a small smile wanting to break out as all my granny's conservative church friend's shot Sasha foul looks for cursing. Then, they shot Misty dirty looks as she made her way over to me and sat in my lap after sitting with Andre's arm around her.

"Watch it, you two. You're pissing off the old biddies."

Sasha was about to say something and I was sure it wasn't going to be nice when an older man stopped in front of the couch. I thought he was going to say something to both of them, but he gave me a kind smile.

He stuck out his hand for me to shake. "Aiden. I've always wanted to meet you. My name is Milo Bachelet. You would have met me at the car crash your grandmother got in, but she thought it would traumatize you to see her with me and made me call an Uber back to my house. Your grandmother was a special lady."

I stood up and instead of shaking his hand, I pulled him into a huge bear hug. I may have been a little drunk. "Milo! I wanted to meet you too. I never knew if she was still seeing you because she wouldn't talk about it. Was she happy?"

"Yes. It was my fault it happened. I was supposed to go over there that night. I was sitting with her when she discovered you had a new girlfriend and it was me that suggested dinner instead of me coming over. If I had been there, this wouldn't have happened."

Great. Me and my granny's secret boyfriend were both blaming ourselves. I was definitely drunk. I slung my arm over his shoulder. "Someone get Milo a drink!" I yelled. "We've got some catching up to do."

Milo ended up being a mixed drinks kind of guy. Misty ended up going and mixing him a Bloody Mary. Sasha eventually gave me my whiskey back and Milo and I settled into the cushions.

"How did you meet my granny?"

"Wednesday night supper at church. She spilled red beans in my lap and bless that woman, she tried to clean it off until she realized she was giving me a crotch massage. I asked her out right after she stopped blushing."

I roared with laughter and the church biddies shot me disapproving looks again. Milo just pat my shoulder. "Get it out, son. Just ignore them. You know your grandmother thought you were too young to think of her dating?"

"Yeah, I kind of figured. Misty here is the only girl

I've dated she ever liked. She was so happy that night I drove her home," I said, my eyes starting to water. Misty snuggled into my chest and I drunkenly threw my arm around her.

"I'll admit, I don't understand what kind of relationship you seem to have here, but when you have a girl that makes you happy, you hold onto her. I still wish I had been there that night." Now Milo's eyes were starting to water.

"It was my fault," I said, starting to full-on bawl. "The same evil people that trashed my shop shot her."

"Aiden!" Milo yelled, slapping me in the face. "Sober up. Can someone get him some food?" Misty and Sasha rushed off to find me something to eat. "I met your friend Casey and I know he's a cop. If what you say is true, I can help. It's the least I can do for Clara. Casey! Get your ass over here!"

I started giggling as the entire room started to titter because Milo was misbehaving too. Misty brought me a huge plate with dips and egg salad sandwiches. "Eat, Aiden. Please?"

I bit into one of the sandwiches. "Oh my god, Andre, your egg salad is better than sex!" I yelled, hoping to piss the room off further.

"I made that, Aiden," Misty whispered. "I'll make it for you every day if you'll just eat and sober up a little."

Casey, Gareth, and Andre came over looking worried. "Shit," Casey muttered. "He's drinking again and he's pissing people off."

"Let the hens cluck, son," Milo said, loud enough for everyone to hear. I noticed a few people walking out. I think that was what Milo wanted. "Aiden was telling me Clara's murder was related to some vandalism in his shop. None of you know this, but I'm former FBI. If someone is targeting Aiden, I want to help."

"I'd love the help," Casey said, rubbing the back of his neck. "But it would just put you in danger."

"And Milo could be Rook," I slurred.

"Aiden, eat your damned sandwich and shut up," Milo snapped. "I've got no idea who this Rook is, but if he murdered Clara, he's on my shit list."

I couldn't stop giggling. My granny's secret church boyfriend had a potty mouth and he was offending all of her church friends at the party. My head was starting to spin. Maybe it was a good idea to eat all these sandwiches Misty brought me so the room would stand still.

"Can you work from home from a computer?" Andre asked.

Milo puffed his chest up. "Son, do you think because I'm eighty-five, I work off a stone tablet? I got a top of the line Alienware laptop at home and I know how to use it. What video chat program did you want to use? I don't have a fucking Apple product, so don't ask me to Facetime you."

I was trying to cram sandwiches down my mouth and giggle at the same time. Andre looked like he had no idea what to do with Milo. He looked like he was scared to suggest a video program because Milo was going to curse him out.

"Skype or Google Hangouts?" Andre suggested.

"Don't get me started on Google and all their spying on their users. We'll use Skype. I suggest you take Aiden somewhere to sober up because I'm calling in two hours so you can tell me who killed Clara so we can nail their ass."

Nothing had made me feel better since I got the news my granny was dead. I wasn't feeling all that better we had ex FBI on our side, but everything else was pretty damned hilarious. I also knew if I didn't eat and kept drinking, I would go from thinking everything was funny to being even more pissed off at the world. I didn't want Misty to see me like that. I needed to stop this before I got worse or I'd be the one to drive her away.

"Is there anything other than sandwiches to eat?" I asked. "I need to soak up this booze in my stomach and sober up before I hurt the people I care about and ruin this party."

Milo patted my hand. "That's the smartest fucking thing you've said since you got me on this couch and started gulping straight whiskey like it was water."

Milo got up to leave so he would be ready for our call. Andre got up and prepared me a plate of more substantial food. By the time I sobered up, I expected everyone to be furious with me. I was just waiting for Misty to yell at me and tell me we were no longer together. I deserved it.

She didn't. She pulled my head down into her lap and played with my hair.

"It's going to take a lot of time, Aiden, but it will get better. You shouldn't blame yourself. Blame Rook and Serena for being cowards and going after an old woman."

She gently kissed my forehead. I wasn't sure if it would ever be better, but her fingers in my hair soothed me to sleep.

14

When I finally woke up, my head was pounding and I had no idea what time it was. I was alone on the sectional with Misty. I was practically on top of her, crushing her, and was apparently drooling all over her chest. I was a hot mess. I went to get off her and that girl is stronger than she looks. I didn't fight that hard when she tightened her arms around me and wouldn't let me. Her hands found my hair again.

"How are you feeling, Aiden?"

"Hungover. Embarrassed. Mortified by the drool all over you. What time is it?"

"Almost noon. After you fell asleep, Aiden and the others went to his bedroom to talk to Milo. You were totally out when they finished their conversation. Milo is going to put feelers out with his contacts still at the FBI to see if they've ever heard of Rook. I also have bad news. During the blackout at the prison Leo was telling us about before he hung up, Dillion has gone missing.

Casey and Leo suspect someone dressed him in guard's clothing and he just walked right out the front door before headcount."

"Oh, Misty. I'm so sorry. I'll keep Dillion away from you."

"I was saving the good news for after I dropped the bomb about Dillion. Grant said he wants to make a statement if he can be guaranteed protection and have a lawyer present. That's supposed to be happening in two hours."

"So, Grant confesses and gives us Rook?" I said, getting excited.

"Looks like it. Should I call the others? I can make egg salad for you again while they work," she teased.

I decided not to get embarrassed. What was done was done and we were finally making progress. "Get your ass in the kitchen and make me a sandwich, woman!" I grunted like a caveman.

"Oh, really, Aiden?" she asked, pouncing on me. She was trying to tickle me, but she didn't know my neck was my only ticklish spot and she was going for my waist. I tried to just forget about Rook and the past few days. I wrestled her onto her back and started tickling her. Unlike me, Misty was tickling all over. Her shrieking woke King up and he was stepping all over us trying to get in on the playing.

"I surrender, Aiden!" Misty shrieked.

I gave her a quick kiss and let her up. I was starting to feel human again. I was so happy that day my granny met Misty and I carried her inside to sleep. It felt like someone had taken a huge shit on my life as soon as Bishop broke the news about my granny. I'd been alternating between intense emotional pain and trying to feel nothing at all. It felt like the sun was starting to shine again and I was waking up. Rook and Serena would pay for what they did to us. We'd eventually find Jake and Dillion and they would pay for what they did to Misty.

"Come talk to me while I make your egg salad?" she said, pulling me from the couch.

I sat at the breakfast bar watching her cook with a small smile. Even with everything going on, she liked to hum and dance while she cooked. She did it that first day she cooked for us and she was doing it now. It was absolutely adorable watching her shimmy and shake around the kitchen. Yeah, my life was starting to look up. The loss of my granny still hurt, but the people who murdered her would pay very soon.

"What's your big secret with the egg salad?"

"Not my big secret. Sophia, our chef taught me this recipe. She said the big secret was to swap parsley with cilantro."

She placed a plate in front of me and we both ate our sandwiches. I heard the guys come into the living room. They were getting pretty rowdy and I could hear them all the way in the kitchen. They were talking about what a badass Milo was. He was apparently going to be giving private lessons to Casey, Andre, and Gareth and wanted to teach me and Misty too.

When we joined them, Casey was actually grinning like a fool for once. "Granny was hiding her badass FBI boyfriend from us. Makes us wonder what else she wasn't telling us."

I needed to talk about her. I needed to remember

the good things instead of just thinking about that morning when Bishop dropped a shit sandwich in my lap. "Apparently, she gave him a crotch massage at church dinner after spilling red beans in his lap."

Andre grinned at me. "Granny was a little minx. She liked to grab my ass when none of you were looking. She probably dumped those red beans in his lap on purpose."

I held my hands over my ears and started humming loudly. "I totally didn't hear that. My granny was a saint."

We were interrupted when Casey's phone rang. He looked up with this look of dread on his face. "It's Leo. It's not time for his chat with Grant yet. I've got no idea if something happened and Grant disappeared too or he just wants questions to ask him."

"Casey?" Leo yelled as soon as Casey answered and put him on speaker. "They got to Grant. Poison. Shortly after they brought him lunch, they heard a crash in his cell. He was on the floor having violent seizures. They rushed him to the hospital and all his organs are shutting down. He's probably not going to make it. I've got no idea where to look for this, Casey!"

"So, we've got a crooked cook or guard. Do they know what the poison is yet?"

"Tetrodotoxin. You know that wouldn't come naturally in prison food and it's hard to get. You can buy it online, but that would leave a paper trail."

"Leo, we know there's not much the doctors are going to be able to do for Grant. What we need to be doing now is tracking any tetrodotoxin purchases in

Louisiana and try to link them up with anyone at the station or jail."

"Exactly how deep does this shit go, Casey?"

"We aren't going to find out until we trace that poison."

Casey disconnected and looked at me grimly. "I thought we had him, Aiden. We were so close. Rook must have a pretty big network if he knew Grant was going to blab something and he managed to get poison in his food."

I was back to that horrible numb feeling again. The black clouds were back. The man that shot my granny was in the hospital dying a horrible death, but the man who put him up to it still didn't have a face. Rook was always one step ahead of us.

Casey's phone vibrated like he had a text message. He shared all of his emails and texts from Leo and Bishop. I could tell from the look on his face it wasn't from either of them or his mother.

"Was that Rook again?" I demanded.

"Aiden, you don't need to read this text."

"Give me the fucking phone, Casey!" I roared.

Casey just sighed and tossed it to me. I stared down at the text message. Another unknown number and probably untraceable like the first.

"The old lady put up a hell of a fight. I've taken one of your players and sacrificed one of my own because he was going to betray me. I hope you can see you are over your head, little boy. Chess is a game I always win."

It pissed me off, but a little ray of light started poking through my black clouds. My granny fought and I hoped she got some good punches in. It was the only thing that could make this even a little better. Casey started passing his phone around now that I had actually read it.

Gareth was pissed. "I'm not doing this anymore. I'm not losing another game with Rook. Rook took our granny and he's not taking any of you. I'm wiping his board without sacrificing any of our players. We are beating Rook this time."

www.ingramcontent.com/pod-product-compliance
Lightning Source LLC
Chambersburg PA
CBHW031307130726
47988CB00007B/2766